The Harrowing

of

Ben Hartley

by
Steve Attridge

An environmentally friendly book printed and bound in England by
www.printondemand-worldwide.com

Mixed Sources
Product group from well-managed
forests, and other controlled sources
www.fsc.org Cert no. TT-COC-002641
© 1996 Forest Stewardship Council
FSC

PEFC
PEFC/16-33-415

PEFC Certified
This product is
from sustainably
managed forests
and controlled
sources
www.pefc.org

This book is made entirely of chain-of-custody materials

www.fast-print.net/store.php

First published by BeWrite Books of Canada, 2012

This edition published by Fast-Print Publishing of
Peterborough, England, 2012

The Harrowing of Ben Hartley
Copyright © Stephen Attridge

ISBN: 978-178035-468-2

Steve writes for TV, film, theatre, as well as books and poetry. He has had two BAFTA nominations and won a RTS Award for best TV Drama Series. He recently completed a sci-fi film script and is completing a second comedy novel in the style of *Bottom of the List*. A history book on the twilight of the British Empire was published by Palgrave Macmillan in 2003. He has lectured on Literature and Screen Writing throughout the UK, Europe and Asia.

He lives in Warwickshire, sometimes in Spain, loves walking, tennis, theatre and not having to go out.

In memory of my father Ernest William Attridge
Nov 8th 1919 – Dec 2nd 2011.

To Ian + Roger

All good wishes

+ seeing a

the

tennis court soon

Love Steve

The Harrowing

of

Ben Hartley

Chapter One

Ben knew he was in deep trouble. They were called the Nomads, but right now they seemed madness itself. Ten of them at least, with the customary black hoods and steel-capped boots that rang and sparked on the concrete like horseshoes. They were some way behind but would gain on a straight road. He had to keep to alleys and corners and shadows where he could use his skinniness and lightness of foot to advantage since he didn't have the stamina for a long straight run. Ben had to hope too that if they cornered him he could summon an edge that would change things. It happened sometimes, but was unpredictable.

It was a cold night but his face was damp with sweat and fear; he could feel drips both hot and cold trickle down his neck. If the asthma kicked in he might need his inhaler too. He never seemed to be able to find it in this place. Was it his imagination or were there more Nomads than at other times? And did they appear bigger, stronger, more organised? How could they grow so quickly? He stayed at four feet six inches and thirteen years old, but they seemed to grow alarmingly.

Down Shaftsbury Avenue he ran towards Trafalgar Square. There was no traffic. It had all disappeared as if to make this more difficult for him. No bus to jump on, no car or taxi to stop and beg a lift from. Few lights from windows. No streetlamps. Little fires burned in the streets. Over one, three men were roasting a pig and laughing. The pig's eyes were wide open like pale wet jewels and Ben felt a dart of sympathy for the animal. To be hunted and caught. Or simply to look up one day as the axe fell. The men took no notice of Ben as he ran past. Many buildings were deserted, or if not, you would not want to venture inside to find out who or what was waiting or sleeping inside. Everything felt threatening, as if the very shadows and dirty bricks and grey pavements had a malignance towards him. He looked up and a man's face filled a whole window, a moon face with expressionless black eyes and smooth callow skin. The man seemed to be chewing very slowly, like a cow, and Ben wondered even as he ran: If the man's head is so big, how can the rest of him fit in the room? He passed a woman in a cocktail dress leading a cheetah on a diamond-studded leash. A barefooted man in a dinner suit moved in a slow somnolent dance of circles. An old woman stood in a timber-framed doorway. For a moment he thought he recognised her.

"Gran!" he said and she smiled.

But he couldn't afford to stop. They were coming. Fear kept him running, a sickness in his belly that said: Anything is better than being caught. Ben was weary of running and his anxiety had itself become monotonous, yet the fear of being caught was greater. Everyone he passed seemed both frighteningly familiar yet remained strangers. None would help. He knew that. This wasn't a time for helping, though it might change at any moment. As he reached the Square he hoped desperately that something would happen to alter things. Beyond the square the river was visible, glinting its oily moon fragments, then beyond that the South Quarter. He didn't want to go there. A place of broken glass and the smell of death. Ben hated the South Quarter and wondered why something kept leading him back to it.

He darted left into St Martin's in the Field. It was dark inside the church and row upon row of figures were seated on wooden benches, all facing an altar. A Priest sat cross-legged on the altar eating a cheese sandwich and drinking tea from a cup and flask which rested on a golden cloth. Every now and then he would look up and say: "It's all right, just carry on. It's fine. Just carry on for now." The Priest kept nodding slowly as if his head was on a string that someone was pulling from above. Ben sat between two figures, a fat woman and skinny man, and thought if he kept still the Nomads might not know it was him. The woman leaned into Ben, squashing him against the man.

"Excuse me," Ben said.

The woman ignored him and kept leaning. He was practically being pushed over and the woman's face was close to his, but there was no breath and only a waxy smell, like an old snuffed candle. Her eyes were unblinking. Ben had the strangest sensation that she was neither dead nor alive, but he was terrified of touching her skin to see if it was warm and real, or cold and something else.

His heart was still beating fast, like a bird trapped in his chest, with the dreaded wheeze starting beneath it. Imagining his wheeze as cobwebs, thickening until his lungs could no longer work, he tried to control it by slowing down his breathing; not allowing thoughts of his absent inhaler to panic him. He tried to think of the wheezing as birds that would fly free.

The doors opened and a spear of dusty light broke down the aisle.

Let it not be them, let it not be them, he thought.

Footsteps running, but only one pair, so one person. It couldn't be them, unless they'd split up to find him. But they didn't do that. They hunted in packs. Ben looked to the side of the church anyway, scared to show his face. In the shadows a movement of something. What was it? Fur? A flash of narrow golden eyes that knew him in some way he found disturbing. Then it was gone. He must have been wrong. He didn't see anything. Someone sat beside him. It was whoever had run into the church. The woman had disappeared. A pale tear-stained face, white with terror, and misted glasses. Ben felt he knew him, or more that he should know him. But from where? Here, it was as if his memory became fragmented and had a wilful life of its own, sometimes trying to trick him.

"Help me," said the boy.

"How?" asked Ben.

"They're after me. The Nomads. I'm scared," he said.

"I thought they was after me," said Ben.

"Maybe it's both of us."

"Who are you?" Ben asked.

"I can't tell you here," the boy said. "But promise you'll come back to save me."

"I promise," said Ben wearily.

"And all the others. You have to help them too," said the boy. "See, people don't even trust their guides here any more. Loads of people don't even know who they are."

"What do you mean – guides?" asked Ben.

"See, even you don't know, and you're …"

The boy checked as the church door opened and he stopped breathing for a moment. It wasn't them. He breathed easily again.

This is all too strange, Ben thought. *I want it to end. Perhaps I'm dreaming.* And with the thought came a great lungful of air and a gush of light. His face grew wet.

Chapter Two

Scrap was the best alarm clock ever invented. At 7.45 every morning he sprang onto Ben's bed and licked furiously at his face, then clawed back the covers. It was impossible to say what sort of dog he was. More a yapping sporran, a little raggedy bundle of black and white furry puffballs, with a fringe that completely hid his eyes. This morning it took him a little longer than usual to awaken Ben, whose mind was still recomposing itself and when he closed his eyes he could still see the spear of dusty light in St. Martins.

"Okay, Scrap. Good fella'. I'm awake now," he said.

But he wasn't really awake. Some essential part of him was still in the anxious ache of the dream. It was like having one foot in one world and one in another, and belonging to neither. The effort of getting up seemed immense; his whole body and mind a great weight. He wanted to sleep for days. Sleep but not dream. Unfortunately the two went together. Somehow he managed to drag himself up and dress, Scrap running madly from the kitchen to his bedroom, relaying yapping messages that only he properly understood.

"You look terrible," his Mum said.

Ben sat at the table and tried to look alert, but he was pale, sickly, a sheen of sweat on his cheeks from the effort of getting dressed.

"Didn't you sleep?" she asked.

"Yeh. No. A bit. Dunno," Ben said.

"Make up your mind," said Ted.

Ted was his Mum's boyfriend. He'd moved in last year and they'd probably get married. He and Ben had tried to like each other and failed. Tried for his Mum's sake and failed because they were such different people, unwillingly garrisoned together. Open hostilities were rare, but that was because each backed off when it could get really nasty. A state of mutual unease existed, a truce, a stand off in a battle that could only end in open bloody warfare somewhere down the line.

Ben spooned down some crunchy nut cornflakes. They stuck in his throat like sawdust. He longed to go back to bed and sink into cool sheets and close his eyes, which felt scratchy and sore. He thought of the boy in St Martins. His frightened eyes and his plea for help. Why had he chosen Ben, a small weedy looking boy with his own pursuers to worry about?

"I wonder who he is? I almost know him," Ben said without thinking.

His Mum looked at him, and then at Ted, who shrugged, and yawned.

When Ben took out Scrap for his morning walk his Mum said to Ted: "Something's wrong. I don't know what, but Ben isn't himself."

"Yeh, he's even more of a weird little git than usual," said Ted, smiling to suggest he was joking, but he wasn't.

On the path that led down to the river they met two of Scrap's dog pals, Bobby and Max. Bobby was a crossbred shorthaired terrier, not very bright, but devoted to Scrap. Their owner, an elderly man called Jack, said Bobby could never be accused of thinking too deeply. Or even at all most days. Max was different – he was cunning, probably a good aggressive chess player if ever there was a dog tournament. He was a little mix of anything from a hamster to a dachshund, even smaller that Scrap, but his inflated ego was by far his biggest attribute, and he spent much of his life starting fights with dogs so much bigger than him that often they couldn't even see Max as he yapped and snapped at their feet. If they did turn on him he would scamper off on his cocktail sausage legs and leave Bobby to do the serious fighting. He also considered himself to be a love machine and spent much of his life burrowing under gates and fences to get at the best looking bitches in the neighbourhood, who invariably scoffed at his amorous advances. Jack and Ben followed the little posse of dogs as they sauntered and playfought and sniffed their way along the river, Scrap's tail in the air like a wonky mast and Max probably boasting about his latest fight and love conquest, Bobby smiling affably at everything and everyone. Jack was walking more slowly than usual. At one point he sat down on a bench and wiped the sweat from his head. He was bald on top, with tufts of hair like silvery brillo pads on each side. He smiled at Ben's concern, revealing a few remaining tombstone teeth that looked as if there was little holding them in.

"You all right?" asked Ben, thinking that if Jack died he would have to care for Bobby and Max. Why did he always have to think things would be dramatic like that?

"Just a bit tired is all. Didn't get much sleep," said Jack.

Ben liked Jack because he talked to him like he was an adult, and he listened carefully to whatever Ben said.

"Sometimes I'm glad I'm past it. It's the likes of you have it hard," said Jack.

"D'you mean the world's changed?" asked Ben.

"It's got old. It's run out of dreams," said Jack.

When they got home Ben felt a crackle in the air. It meant his Mum had something to say, something he wouldn't like.

"You'll be late for school today, Ben. I've made an appointment with Doctor Skinner," she said.

Ted smirked behind his copy of the *Sun*. He knew Ben hated going to the Doctor. He'd spent half his childhood in Doctor Skinner's surgery because of his asthma.

"There's nothing wrong with me. Just a bit knackered is all," said Ben, knowing that the look in his Mum's eyes meant it would be useless to argue. The steel had set in her.

In the surgery waiting room Ben almost dozed off. Mrs Hartley elbowed him awake and as he opened his eyes he saw the wisp of a shadow leaving through the open door. The ghost of a grin. A whiff of meat. But how could a slinking shadow grin? And animals weren't allowed in the waiting room.

Doctor Skinner was all crinkly-eyed smiles and liver-spotted hands and seemed ancient. He listened attentively, nodding his head slowly up and down as Ben winced while his Mum detailed his sleepless nights, increasing asthma problems and general exhaustion. Ben was praying to some god of Embarrassment that the Doctor wouldn't ask him if he was having any trouble with Number Twos.

"Not in a good way then, young Ben??" asked the Doctor, turning to him. "Is there something troubling you?"

"Have you got a dog?" asked Ben.

This seemed to disconcert the Doctor.

"No. Why do you ask?"

Ben had learnt, in principle, that it was rarely a good idea to tell adults what you were thinking. They either assumed you were lying or completely off your trolley.

"It doesn't matter," said Ben. "I probably imagined it."

There I go again, Ben thought. *Put a sock in it. Keep shtum. Lips buttoned. Mouth zipped.* But it was too late.

The good Doctor looked at Ben as if he had a large bogey swinging from his nostril.

"I'm going to recommend that Ben sees another doctor. More of a specialist," said Doctor Skinner, turning back to Mrs Hartley.

She looked anxiously at Ben, who smiled wanly.

"What sort of Doctor? Not a … you know. I mean, there's nothing wrong with Ben's … I mean he is … you know … Isn't he?"

"Yes, of course," said the Doctor, reassuring her completely meaningless enquiry, though of course they all knew she meant: Is my son barking bonkers? Is he mad as a maggot? Crazy as a golf course? A gaga loonytunes crack-brained, daft and dippy, cranky wacky, dotty potty, up the wall round the bend lunatic? Ben thought there must be a lot of lunatics in the world because there were so many ways of describing them. Maybe everyone was mad. The Doctor wrote a note and put it in a little OUT tray on his desk.

Had they had stayed in the room a few moments more Mrs Hartley would have questioned the good Doctor's decision, for as the door closed the blood drained from his face and his head slowly slumped forehead first on his desk and he started snoring gently as sleep claimed him.

That night Ben was so tired he didn't bother to brush his teeth or undress. He just crawled under the sheets in his clothes and Scrap curled up on the duvet over his feet.

Chapter Three

"Slammer! He's over here!"

Ben looked up at the black hood and was aware of moonlight glinting on steel toecaps. He knew he'd made a mistake. Hoping there was no dog poo in them, he'd covered himself in leaves and had instantly gone to sleep. But that was a stupid thing to do because things shifted and shape changed when you slept. The world altered its course around the journey of your sleeping. Even as terror at what they might do began to ice up his veins, he wondered: *Do you dream here too? Is there any point in running?*

As his mind seared over the possible consequences of not running, things broken and hurt and bleeding and never put right again, he found a little courage born of fear. He booted the Nomad hard in a shin, then jumped to his feet and ran into the darkness.

The Nomad howled and suddenly a pack of them was after him. Ben was on open ground now, which was bad. His only hope was cover, hiding. He could hear them thundering behind him and whooping.

"Reddog! He caught you a nifty one!"

"Yeah, but I'll well blackeye his noggin when we catch him."

"I might toothbreak him and make a necko-lace."

"You and me too, Slammer. Little dropturd won't get back tonight."

Help help help help help. The word crashed through Ben's head with each step as he ran. *Why am I always scared here? Why can't anything good happen?*

His wheeze started to string his lungs into chewing gum. *Please someone – HELP ME!*

Suddenly the Nomads stopped. There was a low, exhaling growl, like an engine threatening to roar into life, and in the darkness a whiff of meat and a flash of something gold. Then the lights went out in Ben's head and he was gone.

When he awoke; *How many hours later? Am I in the same place? Where are they now?* He seemed to be close to the Thames as there was the smell of the river. Damp, cold, vaporous. His first solid thought was: *I am not dead.* He tried to look around but it was dark although he could see moonlight teardropping the water and a few brave nightbirds at the shore. He was under a tree at river level, but the tide was out and had left a lot of debris. Again he could smell meat. It wasn't pleasant. Then he heard something – a snuffling, a pulling apart. A little away something was alive. Ben thought of running, but where? He'd have to climb up to get on the Thames path. In the dark something flashed gold.

"Who's there?" Ben asked.

"You is," someone, or something answered, but it wasn't a human voice, more a kind of growl.

The clouds parted like theatre curtains and in the pale moonlight Ben's spit dried in his mouth as he saw, less than three metres away, a kind of animal lying on its belly, its front paws extended and holding something glistening and meaty, maybe a rat. The animal could have been a crossbreed wolf. It had short stiff ears, a muzzle of ragged fur, and a long snout that was pulled back in what looked like a sneer, and thin eyes rimmed with a reddish gold. The eyes seemed to slide in its head, taking in but never directly looking at Ben, as if the creature was constantly looking in the middle distance for something hostile.

"Thought you'd never shout," said the creature.

"Shout what?" asked Ben, wondering if he was the next course for supper.

"Help help help help," said the creature, sneering slightly, then he pulled a bit of something gristly from whatever he was holding and swallowed it whole.

"What are you eating?" asked Ben, curiosity overcoming fear.

"Something. Scuttler or wigbat or suchlike. Didn't look too close when I snatched it. You wanna eat with the Wolf?" Here some sort of wheezy chuckle shook in his chest. "Chickadee, you must be lonely. One hell lonely. I mean, I don't tuxedo up for grubbing. It's kinda quick. There's the food, usually it's dead, then it's gone."

"No thanks. I'm not that hungry. I've seen you before. At least I think I have, or a bit of you," said Ben.

"Yeah, me get about a bit. Name's Wolf."

"Was it you saved me from them?"

"Nomads? Yeah. Them's got it in for us but me don't give a leg shake. Me give 'em a bit of hardeye, tooth-show, stiff fur-crackle. That scare 'em up a bit. Give 'em hardeye big wolflook." And to demonstrate Wolf suddenly turned his eyes on Ben for the first time. Ben gasped as the eyes widened and deepened and seemed about to suck Ben in to some dark, fiery place. He thought he could hear screams from somewhere. Wolf looked away and chuckled, then belched loudly. The meal was finished. From somewhere he then produced a slightly bent cheroot-type cigar and deftly put it in his mouth, clenched on one side between his teeth. Then he scratched a stone with his front left paw and a spark leapt to the cigar. He took a long draw then exhaled a plume of yellow smoke.

"After grub a good choke on a smoke," growled Wolf.

"Smoking's really bad for you," said Ben, feeling his own chest tighten as the smoke drifted towards him.

"Yeah yeah, goody two shoes. You a good sally army church boy. Look at me all holy holy ha ha ha help help help. You got stuff happening here make smoking seem like a whiff of heaven."

Despite his fear Ben was intrigued by this character.

"How come you can talk?" he asked.

"'Cos it's the only way a brainturd like you can listen."

"Who are those people who keep chasing me?" he asked.

"The Nomads? DreamTown losers. Notbright. They be the Longtimers stuck here. Hate you 'cos you get out sometimes."

"You mean when I wake up?"

"Wake up from what, chickadee? That's the prob now. But too many questions. I got to get you to see The Mathematician – he needs to put you straight before you get ready for the Harrowing."

"I don't understand," said Ben.

"I'll make it simple. You got the gift. Look on your arm," said the Wolf.

Ben didn't need to look. There was a tiny red pentagram on his right forearm, a birthmark. It meant nothing. At least, it hadn't until now.

"You rub that thing, I'll know. Be more easytime than all that running help help help. You rub it, I'll be around if I can. Time to go. He's waiting." Wolf spat the thin cigar into the mud, where it spluttered out, then closed his eyes, and a faint breeze started. Ben seemed to blank out for a moment and when he came to he and Wolf were on the Thames Path, Wolf trotting a few metres ahead of him. Ben tried to catch up, partly because he was downwind of Wolf, who was quite smelly: a pot pourri of decaying leaves, undercooked meat, cigar smoke and something else Ben preferred not to think about. They crossed Hammersmith Bridge on the left and Ben had a familiar feeling of going South, which he always hated. It seemed a place of dread. Once over the bridge they turned left and set off along a path by the river, lit only by moonlight. Ben nearly stumbled over two figures playing chess on the path. One looked like Jack but he seemed oblivious of Ben, who could see he had just made a disastrous move, ensuring his Queen would be taken by his opponent's Bishop. His opponent looked up and Ben started. It was the boy from the

Church, the one who had made him promise he would help. Now he looked older, his face sickly pale. Again, a nagging familiarity about him troubled Ben.

"You will help? You promised," the boy said.

"I don't know how to help. I don't know what I'm meant to do. But who are you? " said Ben.

"I keep seeing dragonflies," said the boy, then looked back down at the chess board.

Ben looked around and Wolf was gone. He started to panic. It was too dark. The trees were bony-fingered gremlins, the river coiled with snakes, the dark itself was liquid poison, and then just as he reached in his pocket for his inhaler, there was Wolf in front of him, never looking back to see if Ben was following. They walked for a few minutes, Ben half trotting to keep up, then Wolf stopped, grinning and giving that eye sliding look beyond Ben.

They were in the shadow of a huge latticed building. Ben looked up and saw large white letters in the moonlight: HARRODS FURNITURE STORAGE. He looked back but Wolf had disappeared and was now in an alley on the side of the building. Ben followed. They stopped at some double doors and Wolf hissed a noise that was halfway between a whistle and a howl. Moments later the doors were opened. Wolf entered and Ben followed, into a dark passage. He could hardly see but Wolf's inimitable smells were easy to follow up some stairs. There was another figure with Wolf but Ben couldn't see who, or what, it was. He wondered what they would find here. Dark rooms. Corridors. Old furniture, presumably, gathering dust or covered in moth eaten sheets. But when the little figure with Wolf opened a door into the main building Ben's mouth opened in amazement at what he saw and heard.

Chapter Four

It was a vast brightly lit hall, with numerous anglepoise lamps illuminating flipcharts, demonstration walls and blackboards; on them, hundreds of small people, adult heads on little chubby bodies, were busy writing numbers and symbols. Equations started on one chart, went across the wall and continued on another chart. Others zigzagged across the room in a teeming madness of numbers. One little man was literally running in circles drawing strange shapes on the floor very quickly. Around all four walls were banks of laptops with little people working on them in pairs. Each screen flashed with equations and symbols. The din was immense, for everyone was chattering as they worked in a frenzy of concentration. If Ben listened carefully he could make out odd snatches of individual monologues – "... square root of 276 is 16.61324772583615 ... the square or cube denotes spirit into matter ... a torch can symbolise self confidence ..." but mostly it was like being in the centre of a beehive on Election Day. Ben turned to ask Wolf what the blimey this was all about. He chuckled his wheezy laugh.

"These Chatterers. They's called the Scholasticals. Number crunchers. They's trying to find a way out by finding a way in. All this prattle make me itch to go kill something and watch them lights go out in their eyes."

Ben looked at the madness going on and wanted to ask what it was all for, but Wolf had gone. There was just the merest trace of cigar smoke in the air.

He felt a tugging at his shirt and looked down. A man considerably smaller than himself was holding a clipboard and looking at him intently, but his eyes suggested his mind was on the planet Elsewhere.

"What's going on here?" Ben asked.

The little man came out of his reverie.

"Going on? Going on? Why – everything, of course. This is the hub. The nerve centre. The epicentre. The vortex, the …"

"Yes, but what's actually going on?" Ben interrupted.

The man looked astonished.

"Where to begin? Where to begin? At the beginning. For a positive real number, the two square roots are the principal square root and the negative square root denoted $-\sqrt{x}$."

Here he wrote on the clipboard and showed Ben.

"Together, the principal and negative square roots of a number are denoted $\pm\sqrt{x}$."

The clipboard again.

"But time and tide. The Mathematician wants to see you."

He took Ben by the hand and led him to a corner of the hall where there was a thick black curtain with symbols and numbers painted on it. The little man struggled to find an opening but then pulled the curtain aside and ushered Ben in, and left. The noise instantly receded and as Ben grew accustomed to the dim lighting he realised he was being observed, by a slightly mad looking man with a moptop of grey curly hair and small, glittery eyes set in a bed of brownish wrinkles. He had several large books open in front of him, charts on the wall full of complicated diagrams and numbers, and a buzzing silver laptop without a keyboard. There could be no doubt. He was Mister Braintree, Ben's Maths teacher.

"Ben Hartley. I wondered how long it would be before you came," said Mister Braintree.

"What are you doing here, Mister Braintree?" Ben asked.

The Mathematician looked puzzled.

"Brain-Tree? Brain-Tree? Interesting idea. An arboreal thinker. Saplings with ideas, branches of intellectual curiosity, thought leaves that grow and fall and replenish."

Mister Braintree fell into a reverie.

"No. It's your name, Braintree," said Ben.

"So you say," said Mister Braintree, who seemed to be known only as the Mathematician in this odd place. "Brain-Tree. The brain symbolises a need to consider our own or the intellect of others. A tree denotes the basic structure of our inner lives. What sort of tree?"

"I dunno. And I dunno what you're talking about," said Ben. "I want to know why I'm here and what I should do."

The Mathematician suddenly looked at him. His eyes became serious.

"That mark on your arm. The five-pointed-star or pentagram. You have no idea what it means?"

"No," said Ben.

"You have the Knowing."

"Knowing what?"

"I don't know. It's your Knowing."

"But if I don't know what it is I know how can it be any use?" asked Ben, feeling this was going to be one of those conversations that led nowhere.

"You'll find out. And your Guide will help you if things get too difficult," said the Mathematician.

"My Guide? Who's that?" asked Ben.

"Wolf. All outsiders have a guide. If not they can't get out. However, I cannot for the life of me see why you were assigned to him. He's ... there's something ... I mean you only have to look at him ... Oh well, things don't always make sense here. But you should know ..." here the Mathematician looked round to make sure no one was listening. "He's not what he seems."

"What is he then?"

"He's dangerous. Sometimes to himself. All I'm saying is – be careful."

"But what am I here for? I met a boy before who made me promise I'd save him. I saw him outside again. He said he keeps seeing dragonflies."

"Oh dear, oh Bovridge and Damerham. Another one bites the dust. More flowers, cremations, ashes," said the Mathematician.

"What are you on about?"

"Dragonflies – the need for freedom but it is short-lived. I fear he is not long for the world," said the Mathematician shaking his head sadly.

"But that's horrible," said Ben. "I didn't want to know that."

The Mathematician eyed him. "I see the responsibility of the Knowing has already begun for you."

Then he told Ben that a large group of DreamTowners, including the Nomads, stupid but dangerous; the Herpies, cunning and dangerous and not very clean; and the Deliriums, Serious Psychos who had never woken up and are now stuck in DreamTown; were all conspiring to take over Waketime, or what Ben thought of as the real world. Someone was organising them, but as yet no one knew who. The DreamTowners were infecting people's sleep, giving them anxious dreams, disturbed sleep patterns, so that increasingly people were always exhausted. Eventually the whole waking world would become so depleted and weary and confused it would just all drop off to sleep, then the takeover would be complete. There would only be DreamTown.

"What I believe you call 'Waking up' will cease to happen, cease to be a possibility, and even cease to be a memory," said the Mathematician.

Ben listened and felt a germ of truth in what he was being told. He himself was always knackered at home, and he'd noticed that a lot of people seemed to be tired all the time. If it was true that everyone everywhere was starting to fall asleep, then eventually there would only be one long dream for the whole world as it spun through space. No life in any accepted sense. It was chilling to even think of. No life. Not for him, his Mum, Scrap, his friends, anyone.

"You've got to stop it," said Ben.

"What do you think this is?" said the Mathematician, throwing out his arms. "That's what our work here is all about. We are trying to understand what we are. We're made of the stuff of dreams so if we can interpret ourselves properly we can perhaps learn how to stop the Takeover. Scholasticals too are the crystals of which dreams are made, and all busy trying to understand themselves. Knowledge is power and I myself am compiling the complete Mythology of Dreams," he said proudly.

"What's all the stuff about numbers?" Ben asked.

"Life here is illogical. Just when you think you're getting somewhere, you're not. Time, place, situation, all shift and change, like a landscape that never keeps still. But underlying everything, even chaos, is a pattern. There has to be. And that's where numbers come in. We are fighting the illogicality of this place with logic. Reason will order unreason. If we can just get to the equation that explains our life here we can stop the Takeover."

"But how?" asked Ben. "You might understand it but how will that help you stop it?"

"Look."

The Mathematician made a shape in the air with his hand in front of the laptop and a string of numbers and symbols appeared. Here in DreamTown the technology was pretty advanced. Laptops had been superseded by Thinktops, which showed your thoughts and imaginings.

"This is getting close. It's almost a mathematical and symbolic representation of a dream. If we know exactly what dreams are then we can make and restore them, thus stop all this infecting that's going on. People will be able to sleep properly again, and if that happens your Waketime world will be safe. Balance will be restored."

It seemed to make sense.

"There's something else I need to tell you, Ben Hartley, about yourself and imaginary numbers. Something very important about your role in this. Because without you …"

But then there was a mighty crash. An explosion that rocked the whole building. Outside the little Scholasticals shouted and screamed and whimpered. Clever they may be. Brave they were not. Thinktops cracked and fractured, their screens like broken mirrors. Walls trembled. Windows shattered. Ben fell over with the force of it.

"It's an air raid!" shouted the Mathematician. "Dive for cover. The Herpies attack us sometimes. They want to destroy our work." A flying shard of glass cut the Mathematician's cheek, then he was gone in a cloud of smoke and dust as another explosion rocked the building. Every brick in the place seemed to tremble. There was broken glass everywhere. The air was a thick soupy grey that burned Ben's throat every time he breathed in. He started to feel sick as each new dull thud threatened him. Boom boom boom …

Chapter Five

Boom boom boom. Ben struggled to breathe as he awoke, the sheets wrapped around his head, Scrap yapping at him and the boom boom of the bedroom door being thumped. Then the noise stopped.

"You got ten minutes to get to school!" shouted Ted from outside his room, and who had been thumping on Ben's door with his fist. "Lazy little git." Ben heard him mutter as he went back to the kitchen to his paper and mug of tea. Ben's Mum worked at the local supermarket and had already left, but Ted never seemed to work. His Mum said Ted had a weak lower back that prevented him from getting a job, but Ben thought the real weakness was in Ted's head, in the part that might think about getting a job. His back seemed perfectly all right for laying on the sofa all day watching telly. Perfectly OK for going to the fridge to get another can of Harp. Wearily, Ben got out of bed. He felt as if he hadn't slept properly for months.

He took out Scrap, who was aching for a pee, then he rushed to school without any breakfast. He was only half an hour late, had missed registration and got to Maths five minutes late. It would mean a detention, and Scrap would be waiting dejectedly for his after school run. His face reddened as he entered the room. He knew what was coming.

"Ben Hartley," said Mister Braintree, "thrilled as we all are at your arrival, how much more delightful if you were here on time. Have you actually been to bed? You look like an eviscerated corpse."

Some of the other kids sniggered, and Mickey Tomlinson, the class Psychodope, even stopped picking his nose for a few moments to snigger at Ben, even though he didn't have a clue what eviscerated meant, nor many of the other words either. Only Ben's mate Tim didn't laugh as Ben sat next to him. As

Mister Braintree started to drone on about the importance of fractions something in Ben's mind tripped, like a light being switched on. Fragments of his dream returned to him. He tried to order his recollections, put them in some sort of straight line. There was something about cigar smoke, and someone very weird who kept banging on about numbers, but then there was a war or something and whoever it was … He looked up and there, on Mister Braintree's cheek, was a plaster. Ben's dream flashed back to him - the Mathematician had been cut on his cheek by a piece of flying glass. It was a coincidence. Things like this didn't happen. There was being asleep and dreaming, and there was this, the real world of school and smelly socks and cars and spotty faces and Scrap sniffing other dog's bottoms and telly and being sick and everything else. There was no connection between them. How could there be? Unless it wasn't just his dream.

"You all right?" whispered Tim. "You look like you just pupped your pants or something."

And this was even more of a shock; as he looked at Tim's pale, tired face he thought, *Checkmate.* The boy playing chess. The scared boy in the church. He decided to test it, half fascinated and half terrified that he might be right.

"Last night did you have a dream about anything?" asked Ben.

"Nope," said Tim, looking puzzled. "Why?"

"No reason," said Ben.

Mister Braintree droned on. Ben yawned. Tim yawned. Half the class seemed to be yawning.

"Couldn't have had a dream anyway," said Tim.

"Why not?" asked Ben.

"'Cos there was one of them wotsits in my room. Wotyoucallem? Dragonflies."

Ben felt the muscles in his tummy tighten.

"I got up in the end but couldn't find it. Hope it got out all right. Dead scary though."

The world was going seriously wrong.

At breaktime Ben mustered his courage and approached Mister Braintree, who was gathering together a pile of books.

"Sir?"

Mister Braintree looked at him. Ben looked at the plaster.

"Sir, I know it's none of my business, but – how did you get that cut on your cheek?"

Mister Braintree looked at Ben, deciding whether he was being facetious or just downright nosey.

"Your concern for my well-being is touching, Hartley. You will no doubt grow up into an excellent social worker, forever poking your nose into other people's business and taking it upon yourself to wreck their lives with good intentions. The fact is, I was attacked on my way home last night by a golden eagle with a grudge. It swooped low, gouged my cheek, then, heroically, I managed to wrestle it to the ground, strangle it with my bare hands. Then I took it home and my wife roasted it with turnips and red cabbage and a red sauvignon sauce. Delicious."

"You cut yourself shaving then," said Ben.

"Your correct surmise thus rendering your need to ask completely redundant," said Mister Braintree, for whom sarcasm was second nature.

"And, Sir, would you mind telling me what imaginary numbers are?" asked Ben.

This got his attention all right. He nearly dropped his books. Mister Braintree was currently writing a very difficult theoretical paper on the very subject of imaginary numbers for a Mathematical magazine. It was his fervent hope that if he published enough papers he could get a job at a University and be free of this ugly, stupid school and uglier, stupid kids for good. He looked at Ben suspiciously. How could he know that?

"Why do you ask?"

"I'm just curious. Really, I am, Sir," said Ben.

Mister Braintree picked up his pile of books and left the room without another word, without a look back, leaving Ben to the swirl of his own thoughts. Those thoughts swirled even more when he came out of school. His Mum was waiting. She even had a taxi running. His Mum never got a taxi. They cost too much. So what was going on?

"There was a letter from the hospital," she said.

"I'm not going," said Ben.

"It was a nice letter."

"I don't care if it had a band playing and chocolate flavoured roses all over it and an Arsenal season ticket inside, I'm not going."

Five minutes later they were on their way. Ben did nothing to alleviate the uncomfortable atmosphere as his Mum tried to console him.

"Ted's promised to take Scrap for a walk," she said.

"Huh! Scrap'd rather have his head put in a liquidiser than go out with him. Scrap'd rather have his tonsils tore out and tied round his neck than go out with that –"

"Ben! You don't give him a chance. It makes my life so difficult."

The cab driver didn't help when he asked where they were going.

"St. Edmunds Clinic," said his Mum, close to tears now.

"Right. I know it. The nuthouse out by Pennyfarthing Woods," said the driver helpfully.

The last thing Ben needed was to go to a nuthouse and meet some crabby brain doctor when he already had more than enough to think about. Tim and Mister Braintree were both here and in Ben's dreams, as were others. He realised that he was starting to think of his dreams not as stories in his head with no substance, but as a place. Perhaps DreamTown really was somewhere and it carried on even when he wasn't asleep, and somehow the two worlds were connected. There was so much to think about. He was exhausted. The cab was warm. He'd had a very weird day. It would be nice to doze for a few minutes.

Chapter Six

Wolf lay in the mud under the tree near the river where Ben had first seen him. He had a cigar dangling at the corner of his mouth and one eye closed. The long jagged nails on his left paw tapped on a stone as if he was slightly impatient. Ben noticed one of the nails was broken.

"Where you been all day, chickadee? I's beginning to think you don't relish my company."

"I was at school. It's really odd because my best mate Tim ..." began Ben, but Wolf interrupted.

"Yeah yeah. You's mistaking me for someone who gives a chuck," said Wolf. "We gotta go see the Hermit before sundown. After dark he big hideaway. Can't tell which is him and which is heron crap. They smell the same an' all."

And suddenly they were on the path, Wolf loping ahead slightly and Ben struggling to keep up. Luckily there was no breeze so Ben wasn't in the slipstream of Wolf's deadly cocktail of decaying meat, cigar smoke, and those other things it was best not to think about. Across the river there was still smoke coming from one or two windows of the Harrods building. Ben wondered if the Mathematician was all right. He wanted to talk to him, to ask questions, even though the more he discovered in DreamTown the less he understood.

They crossed Hammersmith Bridge and turned right along the river path. The sun was low in the West and cast golden slivers on the river, making it look warm and healing for once. Ben was bursting with questions.

"S'cuse me," he said.

Wolf kept loping along but Ben assumed he was listening.

"S'cuse me, but that Mathematician bloke said I have the Knowing. Do you know what that means?" There was no response. "It seems to mean that I know things I don't even know I know. And things I don't want to know anyway. He said it's a great responsibility."

"Yeah? I call it a real bummer," said Wolf with a wheezy chuckle.

And that was all Ben got from him. Perhaps the Hermit would know. It all made Ben feel anxious. There was the familiar tightening in his chest. He took out his inhaler and had a few quick blasts, which calmed him and relaxed his breathing. Wolf took an abrupt left turn down a footpath. After a hundred yards or so there was a wooden fence to the right, then a gate with a notice:

LEG O' MUTTON ISLAND. SANCTUARY.

Wolf went in and Ben followed. Wolf turned right along a narrow path. The path circled a lake with great floating nests like little boats or islands, made of scrub and grasses and twigs. There were four or five young heron in each nest, and one or two bigger parents keeping watch. Ben felt he was an intruder here, in this kingdom of birds. The larger heron kept a wary eye on him as he followed Wolf.

Halfway round the lake Wolf stopped and sniffed the air, then his nostril caught some powerful smell and he sneezed and spat.

"This him," he said. "Old righteous stinko with his greylocks and gasbender breath."

Ben couldn't help thinking that in the realm of personal hygiene Wolf himself could do with a few bars of soap and disinfectant. Wolf seemed to know Ben's thoughts and slid an eye at him, chuckling wheezily.

"Me get in the river every few months chasing up some swimmy Grubteaser for the killandeat. That clean enough for me, Chickadee. Things smell me coming gives 'em time to get scared and freeze up nice and easy for grubbing."

Ben looked at the tangled mass of briars and leaves behind Wolf and slowly saw that this was a sort of camouflaged door.

Wolf gave a shrill whistle. No one stirred. Wolf whistled again. Nothing.

"Perhaps he's out," said Ben.

"He there. Feel it," said Wolf.

Ben stayed still for a moment and, sure enough, he could feel someone's presence behind the thick wall of island debris.

"Hello, is anyone there?" Ben asked.

"No," said someone from behind the foliage.

"Is that the Hermit?"

Nothing.

"I'm supposed to see you. Can we come in?"

"No one here," said the voice.

This was silly.

"I know you're there because you're talking," said Ben.

Wolf settled down and dozed. He wasn't getting involved in this. After a few seconds there was a weary sigh that seemed to carry all the pain of the world in it.

"How can I be a hermit if people keep coming to see me?" said the Hermit from behind his green and brown screen. "I mean, it's ridiculous. How can I be alone if other people won't go away? You can't be a Hermit in a chuffing crowd!"

"There's only me and Wolf, and this is the first time I've ever been here," said Ben.

"Yes, right, and my name's Horatio Codswollop. I bet there are multitudes of you out there, all jostling about with your ipods and caravans and fairgrounds and underground transportations blaring away. I crave solitude and what do I get? Millions of marauding tourists, all gabbling away on their infernal talking machines and spoiling my miserable peace with their wittering and twittering. Why don't you all just chuff off and leave me in misery?"

He seemed to have stopped for a moment. Ben took advantage of the pause.

"I'm sure I won't keep you long. My name's Ben."

A moment's silence. Now the voice was different.

"Ben? Ben who?"

"Ben Hartley."

A sharp intake of breath as if someone had pricked the Hermit with a pin.

"Pull the other one. Ben Hartley? Is this a joke?

"No. Honest. My name's Ben Hartley."

Leaves rustled. Twigs broke. Earth shifted and a dirty, tired face appeared, two infinitely sad, troubled brown eyes peering from a mass of grey whiskers and long matted salt and pepper hair.

"Ben Hartley. You found me. Come in."

Ben entered the Hermit's small home. It was like a damp, gloomy, smelly igloo, with a rounded roof. Layers of decaying leaves had been mulched down for months, perhaps years, and made the floor squelchy and unpleasant.

"Not much, but at least it's not home. The worse the better," said the Hermit.

"What's so great about it being horrible?" Ben asked.

"Reminds me how terrible life is. What a horrible place this and everywhere else is. How disgusting people are. How spiteful and frightening all living things are. But enough of this cheery badinage. Sit down, Ben Hartley," said the Hermit, but there was nowhere to sit, so Ben stood. He looked at the Hermit – his thin arms and bony fingers, skinny white legs in old tattered shorts and a t-shirt that was once orange but was now a map of grey and brown stains. The Hermit was certainly a miserable old git, but somehow Ben felt safe with him.

"How did you find me?" asked the Hermit.

"Wolf brought me."

"Yes. Be careful of that one," said the Hermit.

"That's what the Mathematician said. He also said I have the Knowing. And that DreamTown was trying to take over the Waking world. That eventually the whole world would fall asleep and cease to be. Is it true?"

The Hermit looked at the pentagram mark on Ben's arm and a tear came to his left eye, tried to trickle, but disappeared in a wilderness of whiskers.

"I think it's true," said the Hermit. "But the getting there will be terrible. A lot of bad dreams are coming."

"What am I s'posed to do?" asked Ben.

The Hermit sat cross-legged and picked up a few twigs. He gave them to Ben and told him to break them. Ben did. The Hermit told him to throw them on the floor. They landed in a little pile, all at cross angles to each other. The Hermit looked at them for at least a minute, and then closed his eyes. After a few minutes Ben coughed. No response. Then a whisper of a snore began and the Hermit swayed a little. He was asleep.

"S'cuse me. Are you asleep?"

The Hermit's eyes snapped open. He looked startled, then defensive.

"Asleep? You thought I was asleep? Ha! Shows what you know. I was in deep meditation. I was having profound thoughts the like of which most people could only dream of. Asleep. Ha!"

"Then why were you snoring?" Ben asked.

"Snoring? Never. It was a whistle of wind, a breeze in the elder leaves. Snoring. Not me," said the Hermit.

"So what were you thinking about?" Ben asked, thinking this nutter was probably better off as a hermit because he was impossible to be with.

"Thinking about? Right." His eyes took in the sticks. "Yes. Them. I see it all now. You're scared of the South. Quite justified too. The Hunt won't be pleasant. But then, assuming you survive it, you'll be looking for a big place in the North of DreamTown. Big building. On a hill. It's fuzzy, but that's where they'll all meet, and you'll have to do something there to stop them, when they're all together. If you survive, that is."

This wasn't very reassuring.

"I'm only a kid," said Ben wearily.

The Hermit looked at him sadly. He reached out a hand, but withdrew it.

"We're all only kids, Ben Hartley. Some of us just look a bit … the worse for wear."

Suddenly Wolf was there.

"We gotta shake some leg dirt. Getting' late," he said, his eyes barely open.

The Hermit looked at Wolf.

"There's a big Hunt in the park coming. Ben has to be there. He can do something. Word will spread, and that will help you," said the Hermit.

Wolf didn't look happy. He spat on the ground.

"Risky," he said.

"Everything's risky," said the Hermit. He then told Ben that because he had never been there in his waking life, Ben's imagination may well become over inventive when they got to Richmond Park, and that could be both good and bad. "Your imagination is both your greatest strength and your greatest weakness."

And suddenly the Wolf was several yards down the path, loping away. Ben followed him.

"Good luck, my boy," said the Hermit sadly.

Ben felt he knew the Hermit, but he'd had that sensation before in DreamTown. He caught up with Wolf.

"So where are we going?" Asked Ben

"Eye of the storm, Chickadee. Eye of the storm. But one thing you need to nail to your noggin. Don't trust no whitecoat. Them's fill you with scrug and you get all scrugged up we both likely get our bits topped and tailed."

Which made no sense to Ben, but that was nothing new.

Chapter Seven

Mrs Hartley was disappointed. Doctor Epson didn't look like a proper Doctor to her at all. He had shaggy hair that obviously hadn't seen a comb in days, an old corduroy suit and no tie. His glasses magnified his eyes so that he looked like an alien. She was not impressed. Worst of all he was Australian. She was not at all sure that she wanted him messing about with her Ben's brain. For one thing mental problems were probably very different in Australia. You could tell that from *Neighbours*. They were just different. If only she had a bit more in the Building Society she could have gone private, where she believed the Doctors all spoke clipped, perfect English, knew what it meant to be normal and wore ties.

"How's it hangin', mate?" he asked Ben, having persuaded Mrs Hartley to wait outside.

"Yeah. Good," lied Ben. The sooner he was out of here the better.

"Listen, mate, I know you've been short on the old shuteye lately, and that can throw a bit of a spanner in the works. Anything been worrying you?"

The end of the world, the death of everyone I know, including myself, thought Ben, but said: "No. Everything's fine."

"Nothing bothering you at home?"

"No. It's all cool," lied Ben.

"How about school. Not being bullied or anything?"

"Nope. I love school," lied Ben.

"Okey dokey. Tell you what I'm gonna do. I'm going to say a word and I want you to say the first thing that comes into your noggin. No hesitations, all right, mate."

"You mean word association," said Ben.

The Doctor looked at him.

"Smart kid. Yeah. Let's do it. Right."

"Left," said Ben.

"No,"

"Yes," said Ben.

"No, I meant I haven't started yet. I was just saying Right. Right?"

"Right," said Ben. "Why don't you raise your hand when you're about to start," he added helpfully.

Doctor Epson began to wonder if this kid was playing games with him. He raised his hand and the word association started.

"Home," said the Doctor.

"Tired," said Ben.

The Doctor looked at him oddly, but carried on.

"School," said Doctor Epson.

"Numbers," said Ben.

"Mother."

"Help."

"Father."

"Dream."

"Animal."

"Cigar."

"Sleep."

"Danger."

"Worry."

"Nomads."

"Tomorrow."

"Hunt."

"Why did you say Hunt?" asked the Doctor.

"Because you said Tomorrow," said Ben.

"Yes, but … Never mind," said Doctor Epson, making notes on a little silver laptop.

Twenty minutes later Doctor Epson called in Mrs Hartley. She looked anxiously from the Doctor to Ben. Ben smiled to reassure her that everything was fine.

"That's it for now," said the Doctor.

Ben put on his coat.

"No, I don't think you understand, mate," he said. "You're staying in for a bit."

Ben's jaw dropped.

"You mean here? In a nuthouse? With nutters and loonies. There's been some mistake."

"It's a hospital, mate, and no, there's no mistake."

The Doctor turned to Mrs Hartley and said he thought Ben needed help. He used words like 'Affect' and 'Dissociation' and 'Cognitive dissonance', which neither Ben nor his Mum understood, but which Mrs Hartley took to mean that her Ben had something wrong with his head, and that this Doctor could put it right, even if he was from Australia.

"Just need you to sign this form," said Doctor Epson.

"Mum! Don't let this bloke keep me here!" said Ben, but it was no use. "What about Scrap? Who'll look after him?"

"I will. I promise," said his Mum.

Ten minutes later a tearful Mrs Hartley was getting into a taxi while a stunned Ben was being shown into a dormitory room with six beds. He was going to be locked up with five nutters. It was all going horribly wrong. He had one more talk with Doctor Epson and tried his best to behave like a normal person, but the more he tried, the worse it got. At one point he saw a shadow slink across the doorway, caught a whiff of meat and cigar smoke, and he rubbed the pentagram mark on his arm and said aloud: "Wolf, get me out of here!"

Doctor Epson looked alarmed.

"Who were you talking to, mate?" he asked.

"Wolf. You'd better let me out, otherwise he'll come for you. He could rip out your throat if he wanted to, then you'd just be another bit of grubticker," said Ben, in the hope this might scare the Doctor.

Of course, it was the most foolish thing he could have done, as he reflected later in bed. Now the Doctor would think he was a full-blown psycho nutter. At nine o'clock a Nurse came in with a tray and gave everyone what she called their medication. For Ben it was a little plastic cup of bluish water. She said it would help him sleep properly and make him feel relaxed. Ben said he was already relaxed but she made him take it anyway. As it went down his throat he turned around. Something growled nearby, but no one else seemed to hear it. Ben decided there was nothing he could do tonight, but tomorrow he'd behave so normally they'd have to let him go. In the next bed was a lad called Graham who couldn't keep still. He kept shifting about in bed. On the other side was a lad called Robin who was terrified of dirt. He kept whimpering and calling out for his Mum and had great dark circles under his eyes. Ben sort of felt sorry for him but also wished he'd shut up. He thought he wouldn't sleep a wink in this place, but within minutes Robin's whimpers seemed to recede, as if Ben was hearing them from a long way off. The next time the Nurse looked in Ben was out for the count.

Chapter Eight

There was a powerful yellow smell of cigar smoke mixed with a pungency of something live and bloody just eaten but not yet digested. Ben lay on the little mudbank under the tree and Wolf was nudging him awake. He licked his face and his tongue was rough and had the smell of a thousand meals on it.

"Is this a dream?"

"You tell me," said Wolf.

Ben rubbed his eyes and yawned. His limbs felt like they had weights attached and a tight band around his head kept trying to squeeze him back to sleep.

"Lemme go sleep," Ben muttered, his eyes closing.

"We gotta move. Sun's awake. Hunt start soon and you gotta be there, Chickadee," said Wolf, licking Ben's nose.

"Go way ... sleep," said Ben dozily.

With a blast of meaty, furnacey breath Wolf growled loudly in Ben's face. It was so loud all the birds seemed to stop in mid flight and the Thames ceased lapping at the mud bank. A cormorant who was standing on one leg in a very balletic pose fell over and squawked with annoyance in the mud. Ben reeled back and opened his eyes. For once Wolf was looking directly at him, his golden eyes a deep red now. He was very angry.

"Me tell you – no scrug. And what you do – gumgizzling the whole caboodle down your skoolies. Now look at you, weak as a bum tickler. You better leglock up Chickadee, or we both for the long dark nocomeback tunnel."

Ben struggled to wake up. He tried to stand but now his legs were like jelly.

"It wasn't my fault. It was that doctor and they gave me this stuff and ..."

"Yeah yeah, poor you," said Wolf, lighting another cheroot and looking with disgust at Ben's attempts to stand.

"Anyway, it's me that's knackered, not you," said Ben.

"You still don't get it. You nacherly stupid or you take classes?" said Wolf sarcastically, and started to move off.

"Hey, wait for ..." but then there was an edge, an abrupt shift in what was happening and they were halfway across Hammersmith Bridge. Wolf was a few paces ahead and Ben was half jogging, half stumbling after him. The breeze cleared his head a little. *This is nuts*, was his first coherent thought. *We're going to some sort of hunt that sounds dangerous and I can barely walk.*

"Are we going through the south quarter, where there's broken glass?" asked Ben.

Wolf ignored him.

"Wolf, what's being hunted?" asked Ben.

No answer.

"Who's doing the hunting?"

"Them," was all Wolf would say.

Ben trudged along the river path behind Wolf. He felt so tired, and more than a little sorry for himself, and he wasn't at all prepared for what happened next. Something whistled past his ear and landed in a tree near him. He looked, and it was an ugly looking dart, with dirty black ribbons trailing from its stem.

"Crud! Missed him!" someone shouted and Ben looked around to see one of the Nomads about five metres away, with a little crossbow. He was just putting another dart in the bow when Wolf landed on him, knocking him flat and sending the crossbow spinning at Ben's feet. Before the Nomad could recover Wolf bit deep into his throat. A fine fountain of blood arced onto the path, and a whistling as the Nomad tried to say something, but all that came from his mouth were crimson bubbles. It was as if he had two mouths – one below his nose and another in his throat. Two more Nomads appeared from the bushes either side of Wolf. One had a long handled knife and swiped at him, catching him on his left rear haunch. Wolf spun and faced him. The Nomad backed away, while the other, now behind Wolf, advanced, holding a long sharp stick. Blood was already trickling from Wolf's haunch and spotting the dirt at his feet.

Ben picked up the little crossbow. He wrenched the dart from the tree and fixed it in the bow. He aimed at the Nomad holding the stick and was about to fire when the Nomad turned and looked at Ben. His flat pockmarked face, eyes like black beads, all seemed to grow before Ben's eyes. The Nomad smirked, as if he knew what Ben was going to do before he did himself. He dropped the crossbow and did what he felt he had been doing all his young life – he ran. Ben Hartley, never one to face an enemy. Adrenalin gave his legs renewed strength and he knew he wouldn't stop until his lungs gave way. Even without looking back he could feel Wolf's eyes on his back, knowing him for the scaredy cat he was, and would probably always be. But he kept running.

Ten minutes later he could feel an asthma attack coming on. He stopped and looked behind. No one chasing him. He was safe. Going behind a hedge he sat on the ground, hidden from the path. His lungs rasped and his throat seemed to be closing; he sucked on his inhaler and felt the familiar dust swirling down into his chest and settling his lungs. His breathing slowed; his face and hair were wet with sweat. He put his head between his knees and tried to slow his breathing. As he started to count his breaths, he knew it was only to put off the moment when he would have to acknowledge what he had done. He had run and left Wolf. Abandoned his Guide, or whatever he was meant to be. But this was a dream, wasn't it? Being a coward here was different. It didn't mean anything. In his heart he knew it did matter, though, wherever you were.

You didn't just run off and leave your companion. Shame burned into him. So much for being special. So much for anything. He wanted to howl at himself, at his Mum, at Ted, at his Dad for not being there, at everything, but all he could manage was a solitary self-pitying tear.

Something coughed and spat on the path, less than two metres away. Maybe it was one of the Nomads. But there was the smell – smoky and meaty. Ben crept out from behind the hedge. Wolf sat on the path licking his wound. It didn't seem too bad. He never looked at Ben.

"What happened? Did you get them all?" Ben asked.

Wolf continued licking.

"I'm sorry. I'm only a kid. I was scared."

Wolf stopped and looked at Ben, his narrow red eyes unforgiving.

"You swallow your scared. That's how you gets through," he said contemptuously, as he stood and loped on down the path. Ben ran after him. *It isn't fair. Nothing about this is fair.* Wolf turned.

"Fair is for fairies," he nearly spat out the words.

How did he know what I was thinking? Ben wondered.

"Haven't you ever been scared?" Ben asked, aware that his nose was starting to run and he was close to tears.

Wolf stopped for a moment, as if something in him carried the memory of fear. He shrugged it off and carried on along the path. He was going.

Ben had failed him and Wolf was leaving. He couldn't bear it.

"Don't leave."

Wolf ignored him and continued to lope away in easy, rangy strides, weight shifting from one haunch to another, the gash like a dark bloody smile on his left side.

"Wolf! Please don't leave me."

He could feel the tears smarting his eyes. He blinked and gulped to make them stay back. Wolf wouldn't cry. Neither would he.

"I thought we had to go to the Hunt."

Wolf didn't break stride and was becoming smaller.

"It won't happen again. I won't let you down again. I promise. I'll swallow my scared like you said."

Wolf carried on loping, but slowing down, then one back foot dragged, then he stopped, waited a moment and turned. Even at this distance Ben could see his eyes were golden and he was grinning. He was coming back.

Chapter Nine

Two exhausting hours later they arrived at Richmond Park. They entered at Hampton Gate and walked down Lime Avenue. There were giant oaks that had been there for centuries. Great open spaces and clusters of bushes. Deer ran in herds – four hundred years ago King Henry had hunted them, perhaps the ancestors of these very deer. But there were strange things too – the odd house and street, dodgem cars that ran on the grass. It was all quite weird. Ben remembered what the Hermit had said – that because he had never been there in his waking life, Ben's imagination may well become over inventive when they got to the park. "Your imagination is both your greatest strength and your greatest weakness."

That's what dreams do, perhaps, he thought. *They take something real and then mix it with all the colours in your mind to make something new.* Despite his tiredness and the shame of running away earlier, Ben was starting to enjoy this.

He stopped at an Information sign.

"Hey, Wolf. Listen."

Wolf looked around warily, then stopped.

"It says here there's all sorts of wildlife. 'Deer, swans, grebe, mallards and gadwalls, pike … and even a thousand species of beetle.'"

Wolf looked a down at a beetle, flipped it up with one paw, caught it neatly in his mouth, gave one short crunch, and swallowed.

"Nine hundred and ninety nine, chickadee," said Wolf, and gave a meaty belch.

They turned left to Waterhouse Pond. Wolf took a long slurping drink from the pond, frightening away some ducklings, then he gargled and spat a great gobbet of something yellow at the retreating ducklings. The gobbet landed squarely on one of the little creature's heads and it cheeped in horror and scooted away, half running on the surface of the water. Wolf chuckled and looked around. It was as if he was waiting for someone, or something.

"This place is weird," said Ben.

He noticed there were quite a few people asleep on the grass and it made him feel the heaviness in his own mind and body. It was strange, people in pyjamas and nighties asleep here, but he was now too tired again to think about it. The tiredness came in waves, receded a little then swept over him again, and he had a funny taste in his mouth. *Must be that blue stuff the Nurse gave me,* he thought. He lay down and immediately felt that sleep was a second away but he was wrong.

Suddenly a horn sounded – a long single whining note that started low, circled up and ended in a screech that hurt his ears. Wolf looked up; the fur on his neck stood on end and seemed to crackle. His eyes narrowed to slits and he drew back his lips in a low growl. He looked around then bent down and licked Ben roughly awake. His tongue was like sandpaper.

"Get up, chickadee, otherwise only way you get outta here is with the Reaper. They's coming fast and scuzzy. Them snapchancers. Everything sharp up for blood. Sleepdreamers in for bigtime shakeup wakeup."

Ben struggled to get up. He stumbled forward and fell behind a bush as Wolf pushed him with his muzzle, then joined him. Ben had no idea what was going on. He looked through the leaves of the bush and what he saw terrified him.

Deer scattered in terror as a band of hunters careered across the park. As they came closer Ben could see what a strange and grotesque band they were. Small, fierce-faced men with dark narrow eyes set deep in chubby faces, wearing metal helmets with bright purple plumes that flopped and trailed like bunting behind them, sat like an army of psychotic babies astride goat-like creatures the size of ponies. These creatures had long front legs, crooked at the knee, with thick thighs like giant hams, which they used to propel themselves like a galloping horse, and short back legs that provided ballast. Reddish coats with grey streaks and goat-like unfathomable eyes. They snorted loudly as they careered around, strings of mucus swinging from their snouts. Some of the sleepers on the grass woke up and tried to run away, but the little warrior hunters pointed canisters at them, flicked a button and large nets flew out and unfurled around the prey. As people struggled the net tightened, until they were balled up and caught tight. It looked excruciating. Then the hunters started chasing someone else. A cart came into view and small men collected the wriggling net balls and loaded them on the cart.

"Where will they take them?" asked Ben.

"Just keep 'em in DreamTown. They's no go back to Waketime. Maybe scullybag some just for the crack. You sees 'em floating down the river to them big old dark places, all puffbladdered up."

So if people were caught they couldn't wake up and get back to their waking lives. People were being hunted to death in their sleep. It made Ben feel sick. One of the worst things was that there was nothing anyone could do about it. People had to sleep, and when they slept, they dreamed. You couldn't keep the whole world awake indefinitely. And what was he, Ben Hartley, meant to do about it? And what was the Harrowing that Wolf had mentioned? And what was the Knowing that Ben was supposed to have?

A thin man, grey with fear, and wearing blue and black striped pyjamas, managed to catch the net and yanked it, pulling a little warrior from his Goatpony with a KERCHUMP as he hit the ground. Within seconds other hunters were there and Ben gasped as one took a vicious looking spear with a serrated edge, strapped to the side of the Goatpony, and threw it at the thin man. The spear pierced him through the chest and stuck out like a giant bone. The thin man looked shocked, his face blanched, he opened and closed his mouth like a landed fish but no sound came out. A large stain crimsoned his pyjamas and spread. He fell forward but the spear propped up his body like a crutch, and he twitched for a good minute before his last breath came out in a long wheezy rasp.

Ben was shocked to the root. Then he paled as he realised he knew the man. It was Doctor Skinner. Here. In his dream. And now horribly murdered by these gobliny little hunters.

"I know him. He's my Doctor," said Ben hoarsely.

Wolf continued to look through the bushes.

"He's my Doctor," repeated Ben.

"So you says. And now he's a dead Doc. Reapered and gone, pickings for the linnets, be bone dust in short-time …"

It was all getting crowded as more sleepers were running, getting caught in the nets. Wolf waited until it seemed no one was looking their way and nudged Ben.

"Run, chickadee. We's going to Isabella. Hope she hide us."

Ben ran as best he could, though his legs still felt wobbly. They went along a path towards a sign: ISABELLA PLANTATION and beyond that was woodland landscaped with a stream, ponds and magnificent floral displays. Wolf leapt into a large begonia bush and moments later Ben scuttled in beside him. The flowers were large and yellow, almost like roses, and cast a golden light on Wolf's face. They peered outside and moments later a Hunter appeared. The Goatpony stopped and sniffed the air, the little Hunter looked around and Ben felt sure he must know they were there. The little man seemed to be looking straight at him. Then the tickle in Ben's nose began – it often happened near flowers, where the pollen raged, and presaged an asthma attack. Ben tried to wiggle his nose to stop the sneeze, he gulped a deep breath and tried to hold it in, but just as the Hunter was about to pass on, Ben gave an enormous kerchoo sneeze.

The Hunter stopped and looked at the bushes, then spurred the Goatpony on, who cantered at them, jumped over the bush and turned to face Ben and Wolf. The little Hunter's eyes shone like malevolent pale gems as he took out the net canister, but before he could press the button Wolf launched himself at the Goatpony with such force it knocked both creature and hunter over. The little Hunter rolled over and got to his feet. He started to take a knife from his waistband but Wolf was on him and locked his jaws into the little Hunter's throat. Ben saw the yellow teeth close like a trap, the Hunter's eyes roll and a cough of blood, then Wolf flung him aside like a rag. Blood dripped from his muzzle and he licked it. The Goatpony stood, unsure what to do without his rider, but drew back his lips to show large brownish square teeth. He decided to attack. Wolf met his eyes, then snarled low. Ben felt the familiar nag of fear in his belly and wanted to run. More than anything he wanted to run. He took a deep swallow, then another. *You swallow your scared. That's how you gets through.*

"Get the sleepcatcher," Wolf snarled at Ben.

"What?" asked Ben.

"On the ground, stupid," said Wolf.

Ben realised he meant the canister containing the net. He picked it up and tried to work out how to use it.

"Listen, chickadee, don't be no scuzzbucket, you be sure you savvy that gizmo before ..."

But it was too late.

Oh Bovridge and Damerham I've done it now done it now done it now The net flew from the canister like a torpedo and opened into a giant stringy mouth around Wolf. His legs tangled and the net tightened. He bit furiously but to no avail, and the more he rolled and struggled and bit the more the net tightened. The Goatpony watched, then when Wolf was a tightly packed ball of fur and teeth and rage, it moved in, baring those brown piano key teeth.

Chapter Ten

"I'm sorry! I'm so sorry!" screamed Ben, and then looked up at the Nurse's face. She held a syringe and was waiting for a nod from Doctor Epson standing next to her. As Ben came to consciousness and quietened the Doctor decided to wait. The Nurse stepped back.

"How's it hangin', mate?" asked the Doctor. "Bit of an evil kneevil in the old dreambox, eh?"

Why does this man have to talk like a moron? Ben wondered, but decided to say nothing.

"Yeah. I'm fine. Just a bit of a dream."

"Fair enough. Listen, mate. You get your tonsils around a bit of breakfast, then we'll have another sesh. Sound all right?"

"I can hardly wait," said Ben.

The Doctor ignored his sarcasm and moved away. Ben called him back.

"Doctor Epson. D'you know if my Doctor at home's all right?"

"Why wouldn't he be, sport?"

"No reason," said Ben.

He couldn't eat breakfast. His stomach cramped with guilt and fear. It was his fault Wolf had been caught in the net, and now he was at the mercy of the goatpony and the other little hunters. Even though he'd 'swallowed his scared', as Wolf had said, for the first time in his life, he'd still messed up. If he wasn't scared, he was stupid. The shadow of events in DreamTown darkened over Ben and all he could think was that he needed to get back before it was too late. Unless it was already too late. It was difficult to know how time worked between the two worlds. DreamTown time was different, but unpredictable. Ben began to wonder which was in fact his real world. He no longer knew. Perhaps both of them. He rubbed furiously at the pentagram mark on his arm but nothing happened. Perhaps it didn't mean that Wolf was actually … gone. Did it?

Don't think dead, don't think dead

… just that it was hard for him to get here from DreamTown. Perhaps.

"How'd you know, mate?"

Doctor Epson was looking at Ben suspiciously. They sat either sides of his desk.

"What?" Asked Ben.

"Come on, mate, you can tell me. You asked about your Doctor. I rang Doctor Skinner to ask for your files and turns out he died of a heart attack. More than that, he died about ten minutes to nine. We woke you up at nine. No way could you know, mate. So what's going on?"

"Nothing's going on."

"How did you know he was going to die?"

"I dunno. He just looked ill when I saw him."

The Doctor stared at Ben. Ben stared at the Doctor. This was going nowhere. They both knew that.

"I have to go back to sleep," said Ben.

"You've only just woken up, mate."

Ben said he'd slept badly. He'd had dreams. The Doctor asked what sort of dreams. Ben said he couldn't remember. All he could see as he was talking was Wolf trapped in the net. Wolf at the mercy of the terrible Hunters on their goatponies, closing in on him. It was his fault. It was difficult to think of everything and everyone disappearing, but it was all too easy to think of a something, a someone that you knew.

His Mum visited a little later. Better still, she brought Scrap, who leapt joyously into Ben's arms. While his Mum talked to Doctor Epson Ben took Scrap to play in the hospital garden. His mum had brought one of Scrap's favourite balls – a well chewed, grungy tennis ball that had been in places no self respecting tennis ball should ever go to. Ben held it and felt like crying.

"I've messed up, Scrap. Really messed up," said Ben.

Scrap looked at Ben, one ear cocked, his head slightly to one side as if he was straining to catch the full meaning of the words. Ben threw the ball, but Scrap just stood and stared intently at Ben.

"What's wrong, boy?" Ben asked.

Scrap continued to stare, one ear cocked high, the other at half mast. His nose quivered but his eyes remained firmly on Ben, who thought he could hear a cry, but somewhere far off, as in a dream. Then Ben's Mum appeared and Scrap scratched himself, tried to twist around so that he could sniff his own bottom, a feat he had never quite achieved, and scampered off after the ball. Mrs Hartley had her, "This is all very upsetting but I'm going to be strong" face on.

"He wants me to stay here," Ben said.

"Just for a bit. He says you're not … you know, just a bit … something else. He wants to monitor you. I suppose they do that in Australia. What with the heat and everything. There must be a lot of I don't know what out there. All that outback desert wotsit – enough to send anyone round … I mean make them, you know, a bit … Ted sends his best, hopes you'll be home soon…He nearly took Scrap out yesterday, but you know what his back's like when the wind gets up …"

"It's all right, Mum."

Ben suddenly felt he had to be the grown up here. His Mum always gabbled rubbish when she was upset. She looked at Ben. Her eyes were wet. He'd never seen this expression of lostness on her face, as if she suddenly didn't belong in the world.

"Sometimes I think nothing makes sense. I have such terrible dreams now. Since you started going funny. I mean … and Ted didn't nearly take out Scrap. I just said that."

"It's all right, Mum."

She hugged him. Kissed him. Then she was gone, Scrap yapping at her heels and looking back strangely at Ben. The one thing Ben was sure of was that he had to get back to DreamTown as soon as possible if he was going to have any chance at all of helping Wolf. For once, though, he felt wide awake. Surprisingly it was Doctor Epson who helped him.

Chapter Eleven

"It's dead simple, mate, you look at the old swinging ticker, I count backwards from ten, then you're out. When you come back you'll feel like you've had a month in the Bahamas."

The Doctor smiled behind his big glasses and held up a watch on a chain. Ben looked at it swinging back and forth. Doctor Epson counted slowly from ten down to one, and Ben's eyes closed.

"Right, mate. Tell me. How do you feel?"

"Terrified. I can't see him. Where is he? Where is he?"

The panic in Ben's voice was real.

"Calm down, mate. You're all right. Who are you looking for?"

"Wolf, of course, you nobbit!"

"Righty-ho. Wolf it is. And where are you?"

"In Richmond Park. Where else you crudbrain!"

"Richmond Park. And why are you …"

Doctor Epson's voice faded as Ben scanned the park. He'd come back in a different place, but still near the Isabella Plantation. He ran towards the bushes where they had hidden, where Wolf had been caught. *My fault it was all my …* There was the knife the little Hunter dropped. Ben picked it up, looked at the carved wooden handle. Then he ran along the path but there was a slippage in things and he found himself in the opposite corner of the park, and there in front of him was the cart, packed with nets full of people and animals. The cart was being pulled by a Hunter on a Goatpony. As far as Ben could see there were no others around. He ran up behind the cart and scanned the poor squashed faces. At least twenty people, a few dogs and cats and what could only have been a large moose, all trussed and squashed painfully into nets, and piled on the cart. It reminded Ben of a picture he'd seen of a plague cart, the dead piled like rags to be taken to a lime pit, but all these were still alive. Then he caught a meaty whiff tinged with cigar smoke. There was Wolf's snout poking through a hole in a net, one rheumy eye watching Ben critically. He still held the knife and he cut through the net quickly, then pulled and Wolf tumbled from the cart. He stretched his legs and arched his back, cracking and levering everything back into place, shook his head and gave Ben an oily sideways look that spoke volumes.

"I'm sorry," said Ben.

"Useless as a skugbat in a gisshole," muttered Wolf.

He shook his fur like a dog after rain, spat a yellowish green ball into the dust, then started to lope off.

"Let's go," he said.

But Ben was staring at the cart. All those poor things trussed up in nets and destined ... for what? A few looked appealingly at Ben. With a shock he realised he recognised some of the faces. There was Jack, looking very ill and almost unconscious, and there was Tim, ghostly face with eyes like pale suns. Ben couldn't leave them. He just couldn't. He cut Jack's net and helped him off the cart, but Jack was too weak to stand and fell in a heap. Then he cut Tim free, who fell from the cart and hung on to Ben.

"Thanks. I knew you'd come. They said you'd come," said Tim.

His breath smelled stale, like mould on old bread. Others on the cart were calling out to Ben, or moaning. The little Hunter at the front heard, and stopped. He got off the Goatpony and unstrapped the spear. At the same moment Wolf turned and took in the whole scene. In a few bounds he was there and on the Hunter. He bit hard at his throat and shook his head from side to side, then tossed the little man aside, where he twitched on the ground, the great gash in his throat spouting blood. Wolf looked at Ben. He was panting, blood bubbles all around his chops, and he was furious.

"Chickadee, you one useless numbo. Thick as scuzz crap. Meant to be some sort of highmighty saviour crud. You get me dead I never forgive you. Come back and skizzle your bits longtime. Now run. Forget old headlump blankeye, he nearly mortalised anywayhow."

Wolf looked at Jack. It was true. His eyes were glazing. He was nearly dead. It was also true that they were in great trouble. The commotion had harnessed the attention of other Hunters and two or three were riding towards them on Goatponies, spears and net canisters out and ready. Ben took the net canister from the dead Hunter and, helping Tim, ran to where Wolf looked – a large building about five hundred metres away. Wolf ran at their side, looking back as the Hunters gained on them.

"Jack, I'm so sorry. I'll look after Max and Bobby," Ben called back.

To his left a Hunter was closing in. He could see the little man's eyes, dark indifference in them that was worse than hatred. And he thought – evil is what happens when feeling dies. Ben shielded Tim on the other side, then suddenly turned and fired the canister. The net caught the Goatpony around the head and pulled tight. The animal skidded and bucked. The little Hunter was catapulted over its head, did a few somersaults, then landed with an appalling crack as his neck broke. His head was at a strange angle as the body stilled, the eyes still appearing to look intently at Ben. Two more Hunters were gaining on them. Ben couldn't see how they could get to the building. *This is my dream. Something should happen to help me.* As if it knew his thoughts a voice replied: *This is not just your dream any more. Everything has changed.*

Another Hunter was closing in. Wolf stopped and faced him square on. The Goatpony's hooves made a drumbeat on the ground.

"You keep legpegging to bighouse," said Wolf to Ben without looking at him. "Get inside. Otherwise I skin you with my gobblers. Lunch on your druggled old headmeat. "

Ben looked at Wolf's yellow fangs. They still had blood on them. Spittle drooled and swung from his jaws like pendulums. Ben carried on with Tim struggling at his side. They were about three hundred metres away from the White Lodge at the centre of the Park. He kept looking back. It seemed the Hunter would just slam into Wolf and crush him. At the last minute Wolf dropped flat on his haunches and as the Goatpony thundered over him he bit up hard into its belly and hung on. The Goatpony ran on, Wolf clenched to its belly, slowing it, a hot steaming oil of blood and offal trailed out, then the Goatpony's front legs buckled and it came to a crashing halt. The Hunter was thrown clear and Wolf was on him in an instant. One scream and it was over. But as Ben watched two more Hunters were bearing down on Wolf. He wouldn't have a chance against two of them. Surely not.

"He said to get inside," said Tim.

"I know what he said!" Ben shouted, torn between what was sensible and what was in his heart. He kept letting down Wolf.

So far he'd been told he was special in some way, that he had something important to do that would stop DreamTown taking over his world and everyone he knew. If it was true, and even Wolf seemed to be helping him to this purpose, then he had to save himself. Wolf had as good as told him to. It didn't feel right, but he jogged on and into the big house with Tim. A voice close to him said: "Ben! Listen, mate – wherever you are, I want you to come back! Come back now! Come back!"

"Shut up, can't you!" shouted Ben.

"Who are you talking to?" asked Tim.

And Ben knew exactly who it was. Doctor Epson. As they approached a door was opened and they fell inside. He looked up and there was the Mathematician, or Mister Braintree.

"Now it can begin," said the Mathematician.

Chapter Twelve

Doctor Epson was in a sweat. His glasses slid off his nose, his face sheened damply. It should have been so simple but it had gone completely wrong. Lightly hypnotise Ben then get him to reveal what was really troubling him. It often worked with patients. Once hypnotised their minds were free to make their tongues say what they feared, or were too inhibited, to say under ordinary circumstances. But something had gone horribly wrong. Ben seemed unable to hear anything he said. He sat there in the chair, occasionally moaning and twitching, as if undergoing some intense private drama. When he tried to bring Ben out of the hypnotic trance by counting to ten the boy shouted so ferociously, "Shut up, can't you!" that the good doctor fell off his chair. He called for the Nurse, got her to prepare an injection of insulin to wake up Ben, then he administered it quickly.

Ben's eyes opened immediately. He looked around, startled, and absently touched the sore spot on his arm where the needle had pricked him. Then he got angry. It felt like a bubble that would burst whether he wanted it to or not. He looked at Doctor Epson and felt like spitting in his face.

"Why did you bring me back?"

"I had to, mate. You were well out of it."

"No. You don't understand. I was about to find out why I'm there. And I left him. Again."

"Who, mate?"

"Wolf, of course, and you brought me back, you … skuzzbanger! You cretin! You doperonus!"

"Listen, mate …"

"And don't keep calling me mate. I'm not your mate!" Ben was practically screaming in the Doctor's face, his breath coming short and raspy. And he'd left his inhaler in DreamTown.

Doctor Epson indicated that the Nurse should leave. He stood and looked out of the window, which gave Ben time to recover. Suddenly he felt what he was. A kid. A little boy. Thirteen years old. Scared. Way out of his depth.

"I want to go home. Telephone my Mum to come and get me. I want to be with Scrap."

"You can't, m–. You can't. Not yet," the Doctor still looking at the scrappy gardens outside, then turning to face Ben. "There's too much going on."

He sat and eyed Ben.

"We need to chat. Seriously chat. Where do you go when you're asleep, or under like you were just now? And who's Wolf?"

Ben took a big breath. He told the Doctor that Wolf was someone, something, that he met when he was asleep and dreaming. That when he slept he went somewhere where he apparently has a great purpose to fulfill. Somewhere where there was often danger, but that it had implications for everyone in the Here and Now.

"So – best not give me any drugs or anything. 'Cos they make Wolf angry, and they affect me so's I can't do ... whatever it is I'm s'posed to do."

"I see," said Doctor Epson.

Back in the hospital dorm Ben didn't know why he'd blabbed so much to Doctor Epson. Perhaps all this was getting to him and he was so worried about Wolf that he just needed to tell someone, anyone, or perhaps because he'd been hypnotised. All he could think now was that he'd left Wolf to die.

If Ben had paused a moment longer outside the White Lodge he would have seen something strange. As Wolf lowers his head and bares his fangs, turning his head side to side to face the two Hunters bearing down on him, a bony arm protrudes from a bush a few metres away, the hand holding an old

Highwayman's pistol. The hand shakes a little, then another bony-fingered hand comes out to steady it, takes aim and fires. A flash and a puff of smoke. The retort throws whoever owned the pistol back into the bush, for there is a thud and an, "Oh boggery!" but although Wolf sees it in the corner of his eye, for he rarely misses anything, what he concentrates on is the whistle of a musket ball through the air and the crack as it drills into the skull of one of the Goatponies; the animal's legs buckle, its little rider yells in agony as the beast rolls and falls on him, crushing one of his legs. Wolf turns and faces the other Hunter. Now the odds are more even. Now there is a chance. He grins and droplets of blood glisten on his muzzle like rubies.

Bushes, he thinks, *you can never skuzz what's hiding in 'em.*

Chapter Thirteen

Ben lay awake. In the next bed Graham shifted about restlessly. He kept sighing loudly. Robin was crying softly to himself.

I'll never get to sleep, Ben thought, *and then what will happen?*

He tried closing his eyes and counting sheep jumping over a fence. This was one of those things that everyone seems to have heard about, but no one knows quite where. Ben got to two hundred and thirty two and felt more awake than ever. Even the sheep were bored with being counted.

How can I be exhausted but wide awake?

He tried sending Scrap after the sheep, but somehow Scrap panicked them and they all ran away. When he followed them to his horror saw they were all running off a cliff. From the edge of the cliff looking over he couldn't see any dead sheep on the beach far below. There was no tide, so the sea couldn't have taken them. If this was meant to make him feel peaceful and sleepy it wasn't working.

"This is ridiculous," he said aloud. "I'm more awake than ever." Then he tried to imagine Ted running and jumping off the cliff, which would have been a pleasant thought to help him sleep, but perversely, every time Ted got to the edge of the cliff, he stopped, turned round and grinned at Ben.

"Are you awake?" asked the terrified Robin in the darkness.

"'Course I am," said Ben. "Difficult not to be with you whimpering and slobbering and sighing."

He knew it was rude but he was tired, anxious, and low on sympathy.

"I'm sorry," said Robin. "But I'm just so miserable. And scared."

"What you scared of?" Ben asked.

"Sleep," said Robin.

A pause. Ben waited for more. It came.

"I have these scary dreams. There's things out there. They want to get you," said Robin, his voice flirting with tears.

"It's just an old dream," said Ben, but the floodgates had opened in Robin.

"I don't want to tell the Doctor. He might keep me in here, and I want to go home. To my Mum and Dad. And my room. I've got a play station and two MP3 players, and a goldfish called Harold. And I'm missing out at school. I came top in Geography and Music and Mrs Winchester says I'm one of the cleverest boys she's ever known and she's been teaching for hundreds of years probably and I did really well in a Maths test where you had to match up these shapes and afterwards Mr Perry said he thought I was going to …"

Robin droned on and on but his voice got smaller and smaller as Ben drifted asleep. Robin had succeeded where the sheep had failed, and bored Ben to sleep.

He was in the White Lodge.

"Thanks Robin, you bored the tonsils off me," he said. Somewhere far off a violin was playing a refrain so sweet that it broke your heart to listen even just for a few moments. The Mathematician, who somehow looked even more like Mr Braintree than Mr Braintree himself, and a small, skinny owlish looking man, stood looking at Ben and Tim.

"Who is Robin?" asked the Mathematician.

"He's … it doesn't matter," said Ben, who helped Tim to a large white velveteen chair. Tim sat and almost immediately drifted into sleep. Ben decided to let him be, but to wake him if he seemed to be dreaming. He didn't want to lose another friend.

"Thank all the numbers you escaped from those creatures," said the owlish man. "The hunts are getting worse. More taken every time. Where will it all end? Pleased to meet you. I am Professor Oswald Dawlish, Professor of Quantum DreamPhysics, and Chief convener of the DreamTown Scientific Alliance Project, dedicated to stopping this terrible business."

"Yeh, congratulations, but what about Wolf? Have you seen him?"

The Mathematician and Oswald looked at each other, then at Ben.

"We watched from an upstairs window. We couldn't actually see what happened to him. There was a lot of noise and confusion," said Oswald.

"Why didn't you come to help?" asked Ben.

"We're intellectuals. We couldn't possibly do anything to interfere," said the Mathematician. "We create the theoretical base from which others act. Without us, there would be no action, and we'd fight to the last drop of someone else's blood to prove the case." He laughed.

Oswald looked slightly embarrassed and shuffled his feet. Ben shook Tim by the shoulder.

"Get up. Come on," said Ben, and started to drag the sleepy Tim to the door.

"Where in DreamTown are you going?" asked the Mathematician.

"To look for Wolf. I shouldn't have left him."

Ben traced their steps across the park back to where they had last seen Wolf. It was oddly quiet. Even the birds had gone. Ben looked on the ground: there were footprints, hoof prints, skid marks, signs of scuffles. The grass told its own story of the Hunt.

"Look," said Tim.

He was standing by a bush. It looked like someone had been hiding in the bush because the centre of it was trampled down, and there were three little silver musket balls on the ground. There was also a strip of dirty orange cloth snagged on a thorn. On impulse, Ben put it in his pocket. What had happened? Ben cursed himself for going into the White Lodge without at least seeing what had happened to Wolf. Perhaps it was because he couldn't bear to watch him being torn apart by Goatponies, or netted and dragged off, or speared. Not watching allowed the possibility of hope.

"Wolf was your friend then?" asked Tim.

Ben didn't like the past tense.

"He insults me. He smells terrible. He does all the things I've been told are wrong, like smoking and not washing and eating filthy food, some of it not even dead. He gets annoyed with me. He's not interested in anything I say. I'm not even sure if he likes me. Yes. He's my friend."

"Right," said Tim uncertainly.

Ben scanned the ground and saw a single bloody claw near his feet, and a long weal in the grass where it had scraped along, before being torn out at the root. It could only be Wolf's. Of course, he would have gone down fighting, clawing, biting, snarling. No one would have taken him easily. Ben picked up the claw and looked around. The silence was eerie. Everything about this hateful place turned to ash in his mouth. The air itself seemed grey and desolate. Wrapping the claw in the piece of orange cloth he put it in his pocket. He would keep it with him always, no matter what happened. A line of trees shivered like spectres as he looked at them. Perhaps that's what they were. This was DreamTown and you never knew anything for sure.

The two boys trudged wearily back to the White Lodge. Ben just wanted all this to stop. He was sick of it. The Mathematician and Oswald stood in the same place.

"Nothing?" asked the Mathematician.

Ben shook his head.

"You may take comfort in the mathematical certainty that everything dies. Assuming there is no celestial deity who, defying all laws of mathematics and science, lives eternally, having presumably created himself before he actually existed, thereby both confirming and negating his eternal status," said the Mathematician.

"Don't you ever get tired of your own voice?" asked Ben.

"Never," said the Mathematician, with conviction.

Then the door opened behind Ben, and an outdoorsy whiff of blood and heat and meat filled his nostrils. Wolf stood there, framed by the door, breathing heavily.

Ben's heart jumped. He was safe. Wolf was safe. He ran to him and was going to embrace him, but the reek stopped him just short.

"Where were you?" asked Ben.

"Went downriver. Cool my skoolies. And wash off some of the guzzblud."

"I was scared you'd … I didn't think …" Ben began, looking at Wolf's bloody front paw with the missing claw.

"Yeah, yeah, pretty speech. I's here. Got some help from a skinny bush. You see that Bones?"

"Bones?"

"Skuzz dealer."

"Doctor Epson? Yeh, I told him I didn't want any more drugs. Maybe he won't give me no more" said Ben.

"Yeah, and maybe skugglers don't pupp in the woods. Anyways, hunt's gone. And all this bloodmongering give me the hunger. I need go grubbing."

"I'm glad you're back," said Ben.

As if in answer Wolf raised a leg and peed against a marble pillar. Then he turned to the door.

"You may not find much around here to eat," said Oswald.

Wolf showed his teeth in what might have been a grin.

"Yeh yeh, but less you only like prettified grubbing wrapped in ribbons and bows there's always something with red guts for stoking a hunger. Sometimes best not look just swaller. Even if a bit undead. Feel it ticklekick as it gumslides down to the big warm Inthere. I'll leave you inter-lecherels to it."

And Wolf left, with a sideways look at the Mathematician, who stared after him with a quizzical look on his face.

"There is something about that creature I don't trust," he said. "But to business. You know the basic facts?"

Ben nodded. Wolf's return had heartened him. He was ready for whatever came next.

"DreamTown wants to take over the Waking World. It's doing that by messing up people's sleep and dreams so that eventually everyone falls asleep. They're also hunting dreaming people and once they catch them they ..." Ben stopped. He remembered all the faces of the people and animals caught in the net.

The Mathematician coughed.

"Exactly. Doesn't bear thinking about."

"But you told me you were trying to understand dreams through numbers. And that'd help somehow. Then you got bombed. How's that going? Any success?" Ben asked.

The little owlish Oswald put a hand over his mouth to stop himself from tittering. The Mathematician noticed this and two red spots appeared on his cheeks.

"What did I say? I just asked if you understood any more," asked Ben.

Oswald could barely contain himself. His cheeks looked about to burst and his eyes were almost popping through his specs. The Mathematician turned to him and tried to look imperious and scathing but this just made Oswald worse, and his laugh exploded with a snort like a wet firework all over Ben.

"What is it? What have I said?" asked Ben, wiping his face with his sleeve.

"It's just, just, just the idea of him," here a nod and a smirk at the Mathematician, "and success going together. It's a hoot.

Him and success aren't even on speaking terms. Him and success are like people who've never met and know nothing about each other. They live on different planets, him and success. Different universes. Different ..."

"All right, Oswald, you've had your laugh. And what exactly has your precious little band of dimwits discovered? More black holes? Time warps? Anything that Einstein didn't know about years ago?"

"Actually," and here Oswald arched up to his full height of about four feet eight, "we have made a breakthrough, of enormous significance. Positrons. The whole key to what will happen is in positrons."

The Mathematician looked suspiciously at Oswald.

"S'cuse me, but would someone mind telling me what you're on about?" said Ben.

Both men looked at Ben, then at each other. Oswald was suddenly very serious and thoughtful.

"About you, Ben Hartley. It's all about you. Don't you realise that? Has nobody told you?"

"People keep telling me I have something important to do, but no one tells me what? And it's driving me bonkers," said Ben.

Oswald rubbed his chin thoughtfully. He sat Ben down at a little table, then paced up and down, thinking. He turned to Ben. He told him that it was hard to explain without reference to a lot of discoveries in Physics and a lot of technical and scientific information, but that he'd try.

THE PROFESSOR'S EXPLANANTION:

Waketime, or the world into which Ben was born and mostly lived in, is made up of matter, things that you can see, touch, taste, hear and smell. The Physicists in DreamTown had theorised that dreams are essentially anti-matter. When you're there, you think you can see, taste, touch, hear and smell, but you can't – it's all sort of virtual. To complicate things, there are some scientists in DreamTown who say the opposite, that DreamTown is matter and what people think of as the 'real' world, Waketime, is more like a dream, and made up of anti-matter. In fact, it didn't matter who was right, because if the general principle was true, that one world is matter and the other anti-matter, when eventually everyone in Waketime is asleep and the two worlds merged, like pouring water from two cups into one, then matter and anti-matter would come together.

Ben listened patiently. Oswald looked at him.

"You see how enormous this is. Nothing gets any bigger. We are at the very frontiers of science. Only you can prevent it happening."

"You said it's theoretical. It might not happen," said Ben.

"But then again – it might. Once something's happened theoretically it exists, scientifically speaking."

The Mathematician was scratching his head and looking very anxious. "Why didn't you tell me this before? About matter and anti-matter."

"You never asked. Too busy thinking you knew everything yourself. You Mathematicians – you forget the world around you where things actually happen. It's all pure with you. With me it's applied."

The Mathematician gave a look of pure and applied malice at Oswald, and then walked away.

"He was meant to tell me something. Imaginary numbers or something. Where's he going?" asked Ben.

"Up his own abacus, probably. He'll be back. But Ben Hartley, are you ready for what has to happen?"

Ben looked at him.

"The Harrowing. Without you there we're all lost."

Ben was trying to wrap his head around all this science.

"When matter and anti-matter come together, what actually happens?" he asked.

Oswald bit his lip. Ben had the distinct feeling there was something he wasn't telling him. Something important.

Chapter Fourteen

Wolf didn't go grubbing at all. He had a notion. It concerned Doctor Epson. Wolf knew it would cost him, but it had to be done. He couldn't risk any more accidents, like in the park. The kid had done his best, had started to show a bit of steel, but he'd been all guzzed up on whatever it was the Doctor gave him. Wolf needed insurance against that happening again. At least it wasn't Rush Hours. Between 2 am and 6 am, when there was the most dream traffic going between Waketime and DreamTown, it was an exhausting experience trying to navigate a way through it. Wolf had done it numerous times and, if he cared to, which he probably wouldn't, he could tell you just how dark and strange and threatening some dreams were, even to him, who had seen and done enough to fill dozens of lifetimes. Once he had nearly lost his life travelling at Rush Hours, but that's another story. His paw ached where he had lost the claw, but he refused to limp. Never let the enemy see a weakness, unless you want to lull him into a false sense of easy victory. He licked his paw. He'd heal soon enough. He always had in the past.

The Doctor was in the dispensary. The Nurse had called him to see Ben, who was muttering in his sleep, in some sort of fever, wet with perspiration, and generally distressed. The Doctor thought that what Ben had told him earlier about some sort of Wolf and having a great purpose to fulfill, suggested someone who was losing touch with reality. Possibly a Messianic complex – thinking he was some sort of universal saviour. It wasn't that uncommon, but the intensity of the condition was unusually strong for a child. Grandiose notions of self plus a belief that one is in communication with mythical creatures indicated a deep psychosis. It was worrying. Treatable, but this necessitated a cocktail of drugs, perhaps for a long time until

Ben stabilised, and could be helped to cope with his condition with intense psychotherapy. The boy may never be able to live a normal life. He looked up at the glass cabinets that went from wall to ceiling, full of labelled jars of pills and liquids. It was astonishing that all these drugs could so powerfully change the human brain, modify behaviour, turn psychotic frenzy into dribbling docility. The Doctor was also troubled by a feeling. He had an inexplicable sense that something, or someone, other than sound psychiatric practice, wanted Ben subdued. He ignored the feeling, it was just tiredness, he hadn't been sleeping well recently, and decided to start Ben on twice weekly injections of largactil, with diazapal to alleviate some of the inevitable side effects: restlessness, arms involuntarily raising like a sleepwalker, perhaps even lockjaw. Some people thought these drugs did more harm than good, but nearly the whole medical profession disagreed. And we know best. Better than all the rest. But as if in response to the thought another popped into the Doctor's head. *Mebbe. Mebbe not. But not tonight, Bonesy, not tonight.*

The Doctor looked up. It had been as if someone else's thought had voiced itself in his mind. How odd. He carried on writing notes and working out the right dosage for Ben. All was quiet. Just the tap of the laptop keys and the hum of the overhead strip light, making everything heightened, almost too real, like in an underground train. He looked at the screen and realised he'd recommended giving Ben a stronger dose than he'd intended. Odd. A name almost came into his mind, but just below the surface, like something floating in a pond that you know is there but cannot identify. A name, something beginning with W. Then the lights flickered, the laptop screen buzzed, threatened to disappear, but stabilised. He looked up. A sudden drop in power, that's all. Why did he feel so on edge? When he looked down again something new was written on the screen:

I SAID NOT TONIGHT, BONESY. YOU DEAF OR JUST STOOPID?

The Doctor looked around sharply. Who could have written it? He was alone, wasn't he? Then the strip light above fizzed again, and this time went off completely, though the laptop stayed on. Its screen lit the Doctor's face and cast the shadow of his head like a large potato on the wall behind him. He tripped the switch of the desk lamp, but it was quite dead. Something, a shadow, a flicker of movement across the doorway, caught his attention.

"Hello? Who's there? Nurse, is that you?"

Nothing.

He was suddenly very very frightened. And he had no idea why. Sweat dampened his forehead, and he could feel it spreading uncomfortably down his neck. It was cold and made him shiver. His palms were clammy with it. There was someone there. In the room but not exactly in the room. *What does that mean*? He stood to go to the door but suddenly the door slammed shut and the shock of it made him reel back into his chair again. This is ridiculous. This is a hospital. I'm the Doctor. I'm in charge. And scarily again a thought came back, *No, I'm just a Bones all Alone*. Where were these thoughts coming from? Not me. He stood and tried to walk to the door but suddenly something was on him, like a huge coiled spring, but heavy, furry. He was thrown onto the desk and a large, breathing and terrifying creature was pinning him down. He kicked out, terrified. A chair skittered across the room. A bottle fell and smashed, little pills scattering like sweets. A smell of rotten meat, stale tobacco, damp fur and something else, something unpleasant. The breath on his face was thick, treacley. Two large paws were pinning him down. In the half light a muzzle and slits of red and gold.

"Good boy. Down dog. Good dingo boy," the Doctor tried to say, but his voice was little more than a squeak with a slightly Aussie twang. This was impossible. It was horrible. It was happening. The red and gold slid across his face. He thought his throat was about to be ripped out.

"Oh sweet Mary. Get off. Get off!"

"Shhhh. Shhh down, Bonesy. Ears awake. The boy. Ben. No more scrug," said Wolf.

Doctor Epson almost had a seizure. It could talk. This thing could talk.

"Oh hell. Oh chuffing hell."

"You dose him and I'm back big and dangerful. Then it's thunderbolt and lightning, very very frightening."

"What's that?" the Doctor rasped.

"It's a classic."

"I don't understand. Who are you? What do you want?"

"Let the boy go, or you and me gets busy with the Reaper. You pixilate him with some bad scag and he ain't no good in DreamTown. Maybe get me graveyarded. Then I dibbuk you longtime. Maybe come back and I jug you bit by bit 'til only left is your breakfast puddle on the floor. Some serious guzguttling. Your choice, beardy weirdy duckwit. Let the boy go now. Tonight. He wakeup now. Compiche?"

The Doctor got the drift.

"Yeh. Right, mate. Compiche. He's gone. Ben Hartley – he leaves this hospital pronto."

Wolf breathed hard in the Doctor's face, which almost made him pass out. Wolf sniffed the air. He knew that something else had been in the room before him. A presence. A something. Him. The One no one liked to talk about. Trying to win the Doctor over. He guessed it was happening a lot now in Waketime. He also knew that the effort it had cost him to get here, to struggle at Rush Hour through all the dreams pushing and shoving and sliding their way to DreamTown, would leave him tired for days. He'd need a good heavy meal, a good smoke and a long shuteye. He could feel the tiredness like a weight in every muscle, but he wouldn't let anyone or anything know that. He just needed a rest. But it wouldn't come. Not for a long time yet.

Chapter Fifteen

Ben couldn't believe his luck. One minute he was in the hospital bed, the next Doctor Epson was driving him home. The Doctor had almost carried him to his car, and insisted he dress in his day clothes. The Doctor was sweating, and Ben was sure he could hear him muttering to himself, like a barking lunatic. Perhaps spending all your time with nutters eventually took its toll and you ended up two bananas short of a bunch yourself. Ben was tempted to ask the good Doctor this, but that probably wasn't a great idea. It was dark. There was a cooling half moon just emerging from a cloud bank, and which cast a silvery light on the fields and trees and telegraph poles that whizzed by outside. Most people would be asleep now, some dreaming, some perhaps never to return. Was a hunt going on even as Ben sat in the back of the speeding car? He'd left DreamTown after being told the awful vision of, what was it – positrons? Matter and anti-matter coming together with presumably apocalyptic results, given how worried Oswald had looked. Suddenly the moon didn't look cool and silver. *There's a bad moon on the rise.* Ben felt that Wolf was close, or had been close. He could almost smell him. He looked at the back of Doctor Epson's head. In the driving mirror he could see that he was still muttering to himself. Yes, somehow, Wolf had been around. And he'd left the thought *There's a bad moon on the rise.*

The next morning Ben insisted he was well enough to go to school. Scrap was yapping, still wildly excited that his beloved Ben was back. Ted eyed Ben malevolently over his copy of *The Sun*. He'd hoped Ben would be away for a good long time, and now the brat was back. His Mum twittered anxiously as she absentmindedly put salt on his cornflakes and sugar on Ted's boiled egg.

"It was just a shock, love, you coming back late last night, and that Doctor, looking all waxy and worried. I mean, I know he's Australian but you think they'd teach them how to tell the time and to look a bit normal. Gave me a right shock, I was just in the middle of this dream …"

"What dream?" asked Ben, looking up sharply.

Mrs Hartley cast a quick glance at Ted.

"I can't say. I mean … I don't remember rightly. You know what dreams are like. All muddled and funny. Best not to think of them too much."

His Mum could remember the dream all right. She just didn't want to say in front of Ted. She fussed over Ben and insisted on walking him to school, although she knew it embarrassed him.

"So do you feel normal?" she asked.

"S'pose so. Doctor Epson let me go so they must think I'm normal."

"I just hope you don't go all funny again. My nerves won't be up to it."

They reached the school gates. Mrs Hartley kissed Ben on the cheek and smiled at him. When she smiled she seemed like the most beautiful woman in the world to Ben. He turned to go, then stopped.

"Your dream. It was about Dad, wasn't it?"

Her look said, Yes.

In Maths Tim kept looking at Ben, then looking away whenever Ben turned to him. Also, Mister Braintree was looking at him distinctly oddly.

"What's up?" Ben whispered to Tim.

"Nothing," said Tim.

"Then why you looking at me all wonky-eyed, like I just pooped on the chair or something?"

"They said you was in a nuthouse," said Tim.

"I was. Now I'm not. What's your point?"

Tim took a deep breath. With a red felt tip he wrote on the back of his Maths book:

Thanks for saving me.

"You remember?" Ben asked.

"I think so. I dunno. It's all weird, ain't it?"

"Yeh. Weird is only the half of it," said Ben.

Mister Braintree's voice boomed across the room.

"Ben Hartley. Such a modest brain yet so much to say. Do share with us the spontaneous effluence of your musings with your little Sancho Panza. A few teasingly complex conundrums regarding Copernicus? Something arresting on Archimedes? Stand and deliver, Mister Hartley." Everyone tittered at Ben, even though few knew what Mister Braintree was on about.

Ben stood, his cheeks like hot coals, looking down at his feet. Then he – *swallow your scared* – stood and looked directly at Mister Braintree.

"I was wondering, Sir, what the relationship is between imaginary numbers and dreams," he said.

Everyone looked at Mister Braintree, who, perhaps for the first time in his teaching career, was stuck for words. He gaped at Ben, took off his glasses and wiped them on his sleeve, put them on, looked at a starling sitting on the window sill, its shiny green-blue breast catching reflected sunlight, then looked back at Ben.

"Class dismissed. You're a few minutes early, so no talking in the corridor. Ben Hartley, stay behind."

Everyone shuffled out. Ben sat at his desk. Very slowly, Mister Braintree stood and approached Ben. He looked down at him. Ben noticed he was holding on to a chairback, as if frightened he might fall. Ben had the heady sensation that he was in control of this situation, at least for now.

"Are you all right, Sir?"

"Of course. What do you mean?"

"Just a bit tired, eh, Sir?"

Mister Braintree seemed not to hear. He yawned and closed his eyes for a second. As he did so he shimmered slightly, and appeared to fragment, as if he was made of a thousand tiny mosaic pieces, which momentarily separated then conjoined.

Mister Braintree sat down heavily. He looked pale and ill.

"Tired. Yes. You know, I think I may be disappearing altogether. Isn't that ridiculous?"

Ben said nothing. Whatever was making Mister Braintree speak like this, he didn't want to say anything that might make him stop.

"Now. Imaginary numbers. How could they possibly exist? The source of this difficulty stems from what one means by 'existence'. In mathematics, whether or not a certain concept exists can depend on the context in which you ask the question. Do you understand?"

"I'm trying, Sir," said Ben.

"Consider the question, 'does there exist a number between 1 and 2?' In the context of picking up more than one but fewer than two stones from the ground, the answer is No. But in the context of eating between one and two biscuits, the answer is Yes, because you can eat three halves. You see? Context is all."

"Yes, Sir," said Ben.

He couldn't see how this was relevant to DreamTown at all, but he didn't want to stop it. He might learn something that was useful.

"Imaginary Numbers: it's like trying to understand a shadow. The shadow lives in a two-dimensional world, so only two-dimensional concepts are directly applicable to it. However, thinking of the three-dimensional object casting the shadow can aid in understanding it, even though three-dimensional concepts don't have any direct application to the two-dimensional world of the shadow. Likewise, complex or imaginary numbers may not be directly applicable to a real world measurement any more than a three-dimensional object is directly applicable to a two-dimensional shadow, but they can still help us understand it."

"Sir, is it something like dreams? People think a dreamworld isn't real, but it can help us understand what's happening in the real world. And the same the other way round. One is like a shadow of the other."

Mister Braintree looked at Ben.

"Brilliant, Ben Hartley. You're on to something. I don't think I should have told you any of this. But I don't know why," and he looked genuinely puzzled. "Someone wants me to keep you there. In … that place."

"I think it's something to do with the Mathematician, Sir," said Ben.

Mister Braintree looked around guiltily, and held his brow, as if trying to remember some long ago event that had all but disappeared in his memory. He suddenly looked old and frail.

"There's something else, Sir. I don't really understand it. It's called positrons or something. Matter and anti-matter. And them coming together."

Mister Braintree looked sharply at Ben. He looked like a man unwired, undergoing some private and tormented transition.

"That, as Einstein pointed out, could be a complete disaster," he said.

"Why?" asked Ben.

"Einstein predicted that matter and anti-matter must never come into contact or there will be an explosion of energy. If the two merge the universe will rock with the most devastating bang and both will be destroyed."

The dolloping great fools, thought Ben. *If this world is absorbed by DreamTown both could be destroyed. But how come the Professor didn't know that? How come The Mathematician, who is after all a sort of Mister Braintree, didn't know?*

Or do they know and not care?

Ben looked up at Mister Braintree, his eyes full of questions. But there was no point in asking them. Something in Mister Braintree had suddenly disappeared; his eyes were mere lamps that saw nothing. He stood, with some difficulty, and left the classroom.

Ben learnt later that Mister Braintree went home, refused to eat anything and sat in front of the television for an hour. When his wife went in to see if he was all right, he had gone and was never seen again. He had, as a policeman said, simply evaporated.

Chapter Sixteen

Ben's next lesson was cancelled because the whole school was assembled in the hall, where Head of English Mrs Peacock was going to talk about open auditions for the school play. Ben had no interest whatsoever in English, or in the school play, and he was so preoccupied with what had passed between him and Mister Braintree that he barely listened to what she was saying. Something about a play called, *Six Characters in Search of an Arthur* by some bloke called Pierre Armadillo. She said it was a play that was too old for some of them, but a challenge shouldn't hold them back and the younger ones were welcome to attend rehearsals. She droned on and on in a windy pompous voice until Ben was nearly asleep. He could almost smell the river, the meaty smoky smells …

"I'd like to end by reminding you all that the theatre is the place where we can discover important truths about ourselves. As Shakespeare said: 'These our actors,'" and here she became grand and thespian, sweeping an arm across to indicate the whole world and everything in it,

> "'As I foretold you, were all spirits and
> Are melted into air, into thin air:
> And, like the baseless fabric of this vision,
> The cloud-capp'd towers, the gorgeous palaces,
> The solemn temples, the great globe itself,
> Yea, all which it inherit, shall dissolve
> And, like this insubstantial pageant faded,
> Leave not a rack behind. We are such stuff
> As dreams are made on, and our little life
> Is rounded with a sleep.'"

Ben was on the riverbank beneath the tree, garbage like the aftermath of a tramp's party around him, but something was wrong, something was different. He looked around and everything was slightly misty, except for the things very close to him. He rubbed his eyes, but nothing changed. Then he saw that he was inside a transparent bubble, like a large igloo. There was him, the tree, a cormorant and the riverbank debris. Outside he saw, slightly mistily, the river, the buildings behind him, and there was Wolf, outside the bubble looking in.

Ben shouted: "Wolf! What's happening?"

But clearly Wolf couldn't hear, and Ben's voice seemed thin and echoey to himself. Wolf put his front paws on the bubble and started to scratch, but to no avail. There were just white scratch marks. Ben hit the wall with his clenched fists, but it was thick and strong.

"You'll never get out like that," someone said.

Ben looked around. He couldn't see anyone, except the solitary cormorant trapped in the bubble, who was standing on one leg with both wings crooked out and his head on one side. It looked like a yoga posture that had stiffened into ice.

"Who's there?" Ben asked.

"Me," said the someone.

"Where are you?"

"Here. Behind the tree, acorn brain."

A small figure stepped out from behind the tree and made a sweeping bow towards Ben, his bald dome reflecting the fading sunlight shining through the walls of the bubble. He wore dirty, baggy velvet trousers, leggings, a lacy white shirt covered with ink stains. He had a little beard and dark shrewish eyes that danced and darted everywhere, above a long nose.

"I am the Bard. The Voice of all England, the chronicler of all humanity, the librarian of souls. Will Shakespeare."

"Right. You wrote plays and stuff. Our school's doing a play. Not one of yours though. Called, *Six Characters in Search of an Arthur* or something.".

"Arthur who?" asked Will.

"Dunno."

"And where are the six characters?"

"Dunno. Out looking for Arthur, I s'pose," said Ben.

"Doesn't sound much of a play to me," said Will. "They should be doing one of mine. I only read and watch anything written by me. Everything else is inferior."

"How do you know, if you never read anything else?" asked Ben, reasonably enough.

Will Shakespeare eyed Ben sourly.

"I know because I am a genius. A genius simply knows things."

"You're a bit of a bighead too."

Anger flashed in Will's eyes.

"Humph. Ignoramus. Thou fobbing fen-sucked bugbear!"

"Yeh, right, and if you was a bit more intelligent you'd be a cabbage," countered Ben.

Will took a step towards Ben. He smelled of beer and candle wax, like Ben's Gran often did.

"And thou appeareth nothing to me but a foul and pestilent congregation of vapours," he shouted.

"When they were giving out noses, you thought they said roses, and you said, 'Give me a big red one'," shouted back Ben.

By now they were circling each other like prize fighters.

"Thou fusty crook-pated pumpion!"

"Yeh, well, you're so ugly that if you threw a boomerang it wouldn't come back, toilet head!".

"Thou bootless elf-skinned flirt-gill!" said Will, his cheeks inflamed.

"You got a face like a camel's bum!" said Ben, aware that he wasn't quite as witty as Will, but was holding his own nevertheless.

"Thou gleeking, unmuzzled, sheep-biting canker-blossom!"

"Right. And when they was giving out heads, you thought they said sheds, so you said, 'I'd like a nice big wooden one!'"

"Bottled spider! Cream-faced loon!"

Then he laughed.

"What's so funny?" Ben asked.

"Because I want to celebrate. You stood up for yourself. Good. Remember that in future. Language is a weapon. It can get you into and out of all kinds of trouble."

Ben looked around at the walls of the bubble.

"Could it get me out of here?" he asked.

"Try. Improvise," said Will.

"What does improvise mean?"

"I despair at modern education. Use your imagination. Think. Paint pictures in your mind. Improvise."

Ben looked around. He went to the wall of the bubble. He imagined a door.

"There's a door here. I'm going to open it," he said, reaching out a hand.

"Ah, but it's bolted on the outside," said Will.

"Then I'll ask my friend outside to unbolt it."

"Alas, he cannot hear you."

Ben thought again. He reached up.

"But here's a window, and I can reach the latch …"

"Which, alack, is broken …"

"Here, a ladder leading up to a loft …"

"The third and fourth rungs missing …"

Ben thought. He put out his hands as if opening something.

"Here," he said, "is a toolbox. Inside, look – a hammer. I take it out and will crack open the wall" He started hammering the wall.

"Agh! As you hit your thumb. The pain. The hammer falls," said Will, and Ben sucked his thumb, which really seemed to be throbbing.

Ben took something from his pocket. He imagined a small state of the art mobile phone.

"A phone. I dial a number. Within moments the fire brigade will arrive with large axes and get me out," said Ben, starting to dial.

Will looked puzzled.

"Fone. What is Fone?"

"It's a modern thing. A device for talking to people over a great distance."

"Ah. 'Fraid not. Out there – the modern world. In here the sixteenth century. No phone."

Ben thought again. He looked at the cormorant, who was in a thoroughly bad mood and pacing around the perimeter of the igloo and pecking at it occasionally. Ben looked up. He pointed at the misty sky.

"There," he said, "see them? A thousand cormorants flying down. The sky's getting black with them. Dots all getting bigger. No, must be five thousand, and what's that? See? They've all landed and are pecking at the ground outside. Five thousand come to rescue one."

He could see them now. Thousands of busy little bodies pecking determinedly like a well drilled army. He could see their prehistoric eyes through the wall of the igloo. Even Will had cocked his head to one side, as if he could hear the faint peck peck peck outside.

"Now. Look at 'em. They can get their beaks under the walls. Their wings starting to flap. See?"

And he could see it happening. It was as real as anything else. And extraordinarily, the igloo bubble started to wobble, then, shakily at first, lift from the ground as thousands of birds put their combined effort to work. The bubble lifted several feet off the ground and hovered like an engine just ticking over. Ben turned to Will, who was smiling.

"And now you are free," said Will. "Don't forget this. It's all dreams and it's all real. Improvise your way out of danger when you can. To suffer the slings and arrows of outrageous ... how does it go? Oh, that's the trouble with being a genius. When you say so many brilliant things how can you be expected to remember them all? Let's see ... the thousand natural socks that flesh is heir to. No, not socks. Shocks. Anyway, you get the main point?"

"Er, I think so. Improvise. Everything's real and a dream, language is a weapon," said Ben.

And as if someone switched off a light, Will was gone, and high above Ben the bubble was growing smaller and smaller. He could smell the river, hear the lap of water. Wolf was lying on his front paws, smoking a cheroot and watching him. He tapped his front paw on a stone, as if applauding.

"What was all that about?" asked Ben.

"Maybe you was only half here, Bubble boy. Not dreamsleeping proper. Maybe that old Shakelegs give you something too. How I know? And a bad moon still rising. The Harrowing. Long Goodnight for some. Ciao."

"Ouch!" said Ben, as Ms Longridge, the Chemistry teacher, gave him another hearty slap around the face. A circle of faces looked down at him, as he lay sprawled on the hall floor.

"What happened?" he asked.

"You sort of fainted," said a boy.

"Like a girl," said psychodope Mickey Tomlinson.

So I was gone but not properly asleep, thought Ben, Wolf's last words echoing in him mind: And a bad moon still rising. The Harrowing. Long Goodnight for some. Ciao.

Chapter Seventeen

On Ben's way home from school he called in at Jack's house. Jack lived in a basement with Bobby and Max. The Landlady opened the door, her eyes red from crying. Ben had half expected more bad news.

"Is Jack there?"

His Landlady shook her head.

"Yesterday. He was taken poorly. I come down 'cos I heard the *News* on telly and I know he can't stand watching it, too depressing he said, so I knew something was wrong. His lips were bluish. Wouldn't let me call a doctor, then he got so bad I had to. He died in the ambulance. Heart attack, they said. Bobby and Max won't eat, won't go out, as if they're hoping he'll come back," she said, a tear spilling on her cheek.

"Can I see them?" Ben asked.

She showed Ben in. He went down the narrow stairs to Jack's room. Bobby sat at the door looking up, waiting for Jack. Max lay on the bed, raggedy head on his little paws, staring at nothing. He gave a half wag as Ben entered, but with no enthusiasm. Ben ruffled Bobby's ears, then sat on the bed with Max. He'd promised Jack he'd look after them. He promised.

"If you like, I'll take them home with me. They love my dog Scrap," he said.

The Landlady smiled wanly.

"Very kind of you, dear, but I'll be all right. I'd like to look after them. For him. For Jack. He was a good man."

Ben turned to go. The Landlady called him back.

"Is your name Ben?"

He nodded. She fumbled in her apron and brought out a crumpled envelope, which she gave to Ben.

Dear Ben,
Thanks for trying. It's all any of us can do. Do take care, if you can. What's that old song? – There's a bad

*moon on the rise. Bring Scrap and come and see Bobby
and Max sometimes.*
   Your friend,
   Jack

A bad moon on the rise. That thought was spreading. And
it was full moon in a few days. Ben promised to take the two
dogs out sometimes, then left, heavyhearted and full of dark
thoughts. He wandered down to the river where he had so
often met Jack, where the two of them had laughed at the three
dogs and talked about life and Jack had always treated Ben as
if what he said mattered. Now he was gone. This terrible crisis
between DreamTown and WakeTime, as Ben now thought of
the waking world, had caused it. It wasn't fair. Dreams should
be about giant tortoises that smile, and kicking a ball that never
gets lost and always thumps in the back of the net, and about
coloured kites that never get caught in trees and always fly,
and watching dolphins and perfect moments that you know
will stay forever in the cinema in your head if you close your
eyes tight. They shouldn't be about asthma and death, fear and
bewilderment, running until you're exhausted and no one to
trust. Except perhaps Wolf.

   When Ben got home Scrap jumped up and twirled in the
air like a mad ballerina, and Ben made a fuss of him and told
him about Jack. Ben was so preoccupied he didn't realise at
first that something was very wrong when he went in the
living room.

   Ted was slumped in front of the telly, a can of Harp lager
resting on his belly, rising up and down with his breathing.
Nothing unusual in that – it was Ted's favourite position, doing
absolutely nothing. He was snoring lightly, and his bottom lip
twitched, as if he was trying to form words but the effort was
too much. Clearly he was dreaming. Given that Ted was the
laziest man Ben had ever met; he wondered what on earth Ted

could dream about. He probably dreamed about sleeping. If Ted got caught on one of the Hunts he'd disappear from Ben's life altogether. It was a delicious thought.

The news channel was on, which was odd, because the only news Ted was ever interested in was that dinner was ready, or his Social Security cheque had arrived. There was something peculiar about the Newsreader. Every now and then his face distorted, as if something was pulling his head out of shape from inside. *Telly must be on the blink,* thought Ben. Then he listened carefully. At first it sounded like fragments of gibberish between real news items, then Ben could make out words and phrases that shouldn't be there, that were coming from somewhere else:

> *Thirteen people killed when a light aircraft crashed in Indonesia … Sleep deeply tonight … The Prime Minister has warned that taxes will have to rise again … Dream of the sea, the sea … Another superbug has broken out in a hospital in Leicestershire … Don't wake up … Go to the sea, the sea …*

Ben couldn't quite believe what he was watching and hearing. He looked down at Scrap, who looked back at him and cocked one ear as if he understood something important was happening. What was it? Some sort of hypnosis, lulling people into a sleep and a terrible dream from which they would never awaken. Perhaps this is what happened to Jack, and if it was happening everywhere then it would be affecting thousands, millions of people. People had to be stopped from watching the *News*. Ben grabbed the remote and switched channels. A daft TV Chef with a little red beard that squiggled up and down like a mouse on a see saw as he talked, was burbling on about making an omelette. Ben was just about to switch again when he stopped and listened carefully:

... Three eggs are sufficient for two people. You must make sure you whisk them properly ... go to sleep soon and dream deeply ... a pinch of pepper and one of parsley to flavour and season ... Everyone must dream of the sea. When you arrive you will know what to do ... make sure the pan is nice and hot and not too much oil ... the sea the sea ... sprinkle some cheese on top when it's bubbling nicely ... go to the sea ... you don't want to burn the underside, so keep it moving in the pan ... the sea the sea ... a minute or so is enough ... If you see Ben Hartley capture him, get him ... the big day is coming soon ...

Ben picked up his Mum's favourite green vase and hurled it as hard as he could at the television. A loud crack like thunder echoed in the room, then the television seemed to collapse into itself, before spitting shards of glass onto the carpet. The vase shattered like a jigsaw puzzle. Ted awoke in a panic, looking around stupidly, seeing Ben, seeing the vase and the shattered glass on the floor.

"What the hell ...? You little creep!" he said and got up from the chair, beer spilling down his trousers.

He lurched towards Ben, who stepped back, and Scrap growled at Ted and showed his teeth. Ted looked at Scrap.

"Little fuzzball, think I'm scared of a sporran on legs like you?" And he kicked out at Scrap, who jumped back behind Ben for safety.

"If you hurt my dog I'll –" Ben began.

"You'll what? Tell your Mummy. She's gonna be well pleased, ain't she? Telly broke. Her favourite vase broke. I bought that – cost a packet. Her one and only sprog gone psycho. I always knew there was something wrong with you, something ..." And Ted whirled a finger around his head. "You need restraining, you do. Need a bit of discipline from a man."

Ted moved towards Ben, who backed away, and then he stopped. He wasn't going to run from this slob. *Swallow your scared.* Scrap was baring his little teeth and this gave Ben courage, even though Scrap was actually still hiding behind Ben's legs.

"If I need discipline from a man, then you better go and find one, 'cos you're just a lardy-bummed nobbit whose idea of exercise is opening a can of lager. You're a foul and pestilent congregation of vapours, a bootless elf-skinned flirt-gill! Thou gleeking, unmuzzled, sheep-biting canker-blossom! Bottled spider! Cream-faced loon!" shouted Ben, suddenly finding that Shakespeare could be very useful if you wanted to overwhelm someone with insults.

Ted looked bewildered for a moment, not really understanding, but then the realisation penetrated his brain that whatever all this meant, he was being insulted, and he took another step towards Ben.

If he hits me, thought Ben, *Mum'll kick him out. It'll almost be worth it.*

Ted raised his right hand.

"What's going on?" Mrs Hartley said, standing in her coat at the door. Not even Scrap had heard her come in.

Ted turned, his right hand still raised.

"Look what he done," he said, indicating the shattered remains of the vase and the broken television set.

"Don't you dare hit my son," said Mrs Hartley.

"He needs seeing to. Needs a bit of discipline. He fools you and the Doctor, but he don't fool me," said Ted.

"Get out," she said quietly.

"You what?" Ted asked, lowering his hand.

"You heard. Get out. And don't come back. Ever."

Ben knew his Mum meant it. So did Ted. For once she didn't look anxious, or in two minds about everything. She meant business. Ted brushed past her. They could hear him clattering about in the bedroom, opening drawers and slamming the wardrobe doors.

"You all right?" Ben's Mum asked.

"Yeh."

Minutes later Ted came back with an old sports bag stuffed with clothes. Ben thought it odd that such a slob as Ted should have a sports bag. His idea of strenuous exercise was breathing. Ted looked at Ben's Mum, then gave a malevolent look at Ben, and left, slamming the front door. Scrap wagged his tail and strutted around bravely as if this had all been his doing.

They had double egg and chips for tea, then at bedtime his Mum brought Ben a cup of hot chocolate made with milk, and two slices of thick cheese on toast. She seemed very calm.

"I'm sorry," said Ben.

"We needed a new telly anyway," she said, smiling. "And that vase was only an old car boot thing that Ted bought me. Ugly old thing."

"The vase or Ted?" Said Ben,

They laughed. She kissed him goodnight. He took a bite of cheese on toast.

"Cheese. Make you dream," she said.

If only she knew.

Chapter Eighteen

They were on a train. It seemed odd because there was no one else, just Ben and opposite him, Wolf, who lay across a double seat, his long snout on his paws, snoozing, his black nose twitching wetly as if even in sleep he was alert and sniffing out lunch or enemies. The paw that had the claw ripped from it was healing and Ben noticed other battle trophies – a scar that ran over one eye where fur no longer grew, a zigzag wound on one ear. Ben felt overwhelmingly proud that Wolf was his Guide. He was a warrior. Smelly and smoky and rude and weird, but a warrior. Perhaps that's what real warriors were; not clean, sanitised creatures from comics or films or games consoles, but those who carried with them the stink and memory of their battles and appetites. Cleanliness came second to survival.

Ben's eyes flickered like an old film as he looked out at the countryside, telegraph poles with strange tops whizzing by. Then as the train slowed he realised with horror that they weren't telegraph poles at all, but human heads jammed on pikes. A wheezy laugh came from Wolf. Then a yawn and cracks and crackles as he stretched his long lean body.

"Don't give them no thought, chickadee. They's sure not thinking. Nothing in them noggins but rusting steel."

"Who are they?" asked Ben.

"Dreamers. Killed on the Hunt and elsewise. More every night. Nomads, Hunters, Herpies, seems everybody after somebody. Soon be time."

"Time for what?"

"The Harrowing, chickadee, the Harrowing," then his nose twitched. "I smells cheese."

"My Mum gave me cheese on toast at bedtime," said Ben.

"Make you dream big and lively."

"Maybe I'm dreaming you. That doctor said you were just a figment of my imagination," said Ben.

"Mebbe. Seemed more than imaginings when I gave him a visitation and he nearly endangered his jodhpurs."

"I knew you'd been to see him," said Ben, politely refraining from saying that it was the smell that had first alerted him.

"Mebbe I's just a filament of his magicalnation too," said Wolf, looking up at the NO SMOKING sign and lighting a cheroot.

"Suppose I'm just a figment of your imagination," said Ben.

Wolf cackled and coughed a wheezy gobbet of something onto the floor.

"Then we's really stuffed up the Yukon without a grobbit to swing from," he said.

"P'raps it's like that funny little Shakespeare bloke was saying – we're all made of dreams."

"In which ways it don't cut no wind either way. This all you got, chickadee, lifestuff, whatever it be," said Wolf.

The train slowed and stopped. Ben opened a window. The salty, green smell of the sea wafted in.

"End of the line," said Wolf, and noiselessly slipped from his seat, then was suddenly outside on a dirt track, looking around and sniffing the air. Ben left the train and joined him. He turned to slam the door but the train had gone, and there were no railway lines. They were high up on a cliff. Everything shimmered and seemed too vivid – the hills rolling behind them, the blue-grey rocks just in front, then a long, long, drop down to the thin strip of beach and choppy foam of the tide. Beyond that the sea stretched like a boiling living thing.

"Something's going to happen," said Ben.

"Stuff always happen. You can't stop it. Nature of the beast," said Wolf.

Ben told Wolf about the strange things that were happening on television – how it was being used to hypnotise people, or at least lull them into submission. Wolf listened but didn't seem very interested and while Ben was still talking, he scratched himself and walked away to look at the sea way below. Ben supposed that Wolf didn't have much interest in good manners. He joined him. They both looked down at the sea. The movement of the waves was disturbing – not the regular beat of waves and tide but like blue tongues lashing out at the air.

"What's this place called?" Ben asked.

"Sea of dreams. Spend too much time in it you gone, chickadee. Your skin and all the scug in it pulled down for shark grub."

The back of Ben's neck prickled. Something was wrong. On the beach way below were tiny specks, moving dots. A long train of them was moving down a path a long way to their left, then congregating on the beach, as if waiting for something or someone. Ben screwed up his eyes and could see some of the dots were people. But what were they doing? What was all this about? He and Wolf found a path that slowly wound down the cliff. Wolf was surefooted but Ben kept slipping and sending little cascades of rocks and dust tumbling down like miniature lemmings falling to their doom. Halfway down he stopped to rest. He had a blast on his asthma inhaler and Wolf smoked a cheroot, letting the breeze blow ash into the air. When they started again Ben could see something happening below. There were hundreds of figures on the beach – mostly people but also dogs, cats, mice, an elephant, guinea pigs, hamsters, a giraffe and other animals and creatures. Now they were moving, walking slowly into the sea, as if prompted by some current running through them all. Ben watched in horror as they continued walking until the water covered their heads – animals and people. The sea foamed with a fury of bubbles as they exhaled under water, then calmed some way out when presumably

This is mass suicide No No No

Ben started to half run, half stumble down the path. Wolf loped ahead of him and a few minutes later reached the beach. He ran along the surf growling and howling and trying to scare the mass of people and animals back, but it was as if they didn't see him. Zombies. Sleepwalkers. Dreamers caught in their own dreams and about to drown in an ocean of them. Even as he was running to the beach Ben wondered what sort of dreams little animals like hamsters and mice had. And what was making them join all the people who had presumably listened to the TV chef? The message was to people. Maybe messages Ben couldn't hear or understand were somehow being sent to animals.

"No. Go back. It was just some clodhead on telly telling you to come here. You don't have to listen. Stop!" he shouted.

What the TV Chef had actually said was go to the sea and await further instructions. Presumably they had received them – to walk into the sea of Dreams and disappear for ever. But who was behind this and making the TV people give the instructions? Ben picked up a little guinea pig as it was scuttling to its death, but it nipped his finger so hard he dropped it. Then he picked up an albino hamster who was drowning in the shallows, and stuffed it in his pocket. Wolf had given up the futile attempt to stop everyone, but his ears were cocked and his nose in the air. He was listening intently, and Ben listened too. Waves curdled and crashed, foam splashed creamily at his feet, the horrible wet plop of souls walking to their deaths. And something else. A high, reedy sound, like a voice calling from another world. As Ben listened he could feel its power. Haunting, beckoning, insistent. Wolf was looking to his right. Standing on a rock about a hundred metres away was a figure in a cloak playing a black flute. This was the sound that crept through the air like a cat stalking its prey.

"It's him. It's him with that flute. That's what's making them go in the Sea of Dreams. We've got to stop him!" shouted Ben, but Wolf was looking at the sea and backing away. Ben turned and his breath froze. It was as if all these bodies giving themselves up so readily were feeding the sea's appetite. It was a coiling, boiling, living thing with tails and tongues, suddenly a hundred metres high and now hurtling towards them.

"What do we do?" Asked Ben.

"I's just a filament of your mastication, chickadee. You don't know, we ain't got no chance."

It seemed nothing could stop it. Within moments this great living wall would crash over them and they would become part of its madness. The people and animals seemed not to see it, but kept walking steadily forward. Ben felt like closing his eyes and just waiting for the inevitable. He stepped close to Wolf, trying to feed on his strength, but clearly even he, warrior that he was, could be no match for this. He was trying to say something to Ben, but the roar was so loud he had to press his face against Wolf's face in order to hear.

"Know what? This thing ain't closer than when it started."

Ben looked. Wolf was right. The great sea wall appeared to be moving towards them but in fact it was in the same place. And what was it after all? The Sea of Dreams. He suddenly knew that this terrifying, living wall of water was the Sea dreaming itself as a tempest. Perhaps it gained strength from the dead and dying whose dreams it was taking into its own cold, watery heart

> *It's an illusion*
> *We are such stuff as dreams...*
> *There's nothing bad but thinking makes it so*
> *There's a bad moon on the rise ...*

Shakespeare said something about everything being imagined, even life. But what to do? Ben suddenly knew. Stop the music and break the spell. He turned and ran along the shore towards the hooded figure playing the flute. Who was it? Man, woman, something else, something ... *swallow your scared*. Every time he seemed to be approaching the hooded figure he was suddenly further back again. He ran and was a few metres away, then was ten metres back. In sheer frustration he picked up a large smooth pebble from the beach and hurled it at the figure. It struck home squarely on the back and he faltered. The flute music choked on its own eerie song. Ben was suddenly almost upon him, if it was a him. He thought he heard the figure talk to him, but the voice seemed to be inside his head ...

Not now. Not yet. Not here, Ben Hartley. But soon.

Ben felt everything change and the figure was gone. The music stopped. The air less charged. He realised he had been barely breathing throughout this ordeal, and took a deep, sweet breath of sea air. The great wall of water had gone. The sea looked a placid grey green. The people who had not given themselves up to it were standing on the beach looking bewildered, wondering what on earth they were doing here. Rabbits and guinea pigs and gerbils and hedgehogs scuttled out of the wet surf. A large, forlorn bear lifted its great muzzle to the skies and howled, then loped on all fours along the beach and away. A snake coiled and slithered to safety. It was over. Only it wasn't, of course, as Ben realised when he saw Ted looking at him.

Chapter Nineteen

Ted was standing in his pyjamas and slippers in the surf about a hundred metres away. The water lapped over his feet and around his ankles, but he didn't seem to care. He was looking at Ben malevolently. A phrase from something Ben had once read came to mind: the evil eye. Then he pointed at Ben.

"Get him! Get him!" Ted shouted.

Other sleepers stopped whatever they were doing and looked first at Ted, then at Ben. A few large cats looked up too, their green eyes squinting at Ben. Then, almost as one, they started walking towards him, Ted at their head, with a terrible white smile and hatred in his eyes.

"You need restraining, you do. Need a bit of discipline from a man," he muttered, then turned to the others: "He needs seeing to. Needs a bit of discipline. He don't fool me," and a collective mutter started as the crowd of some fifty or sixty shuffled towards Ben like an army of zombies. What had the TV chef said? "If you see Ben Hartley capture him, get him … the big day is coming soon." These sleeping people were acting under orders, though in Ted's case, also fuelled by hatred.

Ted picked up a large stone and threw it at Ben. It missed him and clattered on the beach. This was getting serious. Wolf bounded along the beach, snarling at the marauding Sleepers, then he came and stood at Ben's side.

"Any ideas?" Ben asked.

"Take as many of 'em into the long goodnight as we can, chickadee."

"How about running away?"

Wolf looked at him and spat on the ground. Ben looked around. To their right was a sheer cliff face and behind them were more Sleepers coming at them. To their left was the Sea of Dreams. Running away was definitely not an option. They'd have to face them. Ben felt his asthma starting, like pigeons fluttering in his chest. Ted picked up another large stone and was about to launch it when there was a loud crack from somewhere just to Ben's right. Ted stopped as if his clockwork had suddenly wound down, his arm still raised with the stone, his eyes bloodshot and wide with surprise. He seemed to be frozen in this position for an age, then a large velvety red stain slowly spread across his chest, and he fell like a plank flat on his face. Someone had shot him. The other Sleepers stopped and looked at Ted's body. His right leg jerked out straight and twitched for a few seconds, then was still, and a large whoosh of air came from his lungs. No one seemed to know what to do. Wolf raised his head and gave a long, fearful howl, and this settled the matter for most of the Sleepers, who turned and ran away. A few stragglers stayed, but in a half-hearted manner, kicking pebbles, a few turning to look at the sea, one or two shimmering and starting to disappear. Ben thought this might mean they were waking up.

But who fired the shot?

To their right, in the cliff face, a few metres up, was little more than a hole. That was where the shot had come from. Could it be a cave?

"Who's there?" Ben shouted up.

Nothing.

"Who is it? Who's there?"

"No one," a familiar voice said.

Ben looked at Wolf.

"It's him, the Hermit," said Ben.

"Yup. If we was downwind we'd know for sure."

Ben scrambled up the rocks to the hole. Inside the Hermit was sitting disconsolately, cleaning an old musket, looking an even greater picture of misery and destitution than when Ben last saw him, and if anything he was bonier. He wore the same old tattered shorts and t-shirt. With a sigh that carried all the pain of the world and DreamTown put together, he rubbed his eyes.

"You came to help us," said Ben.

"Not at all," said the Hermit defensively. "Just happened to be in the area."

"Yeh, right. Just happened to be in a little hole in the rock in the middle of nowhere."

"Well, where would you expect a hermit to be," he said.

It was a fair point.

"But you've got a gun," said Ben.

"Pure coincidence," said the Hermit.

"Where will you go now? Back to Leg O' Mutton Island?"

The Hermit sighed again.

"Too crowded. One day there were two people walking around it, making terrible noises."

"What noises?"

"Oh, you know, breathing and wotnot. Horrible human noises," the Hermit shook his head sadly. He was a real mess and looked as if he hadn't eaten for days. "Anyway, I have to go," and he got to his feet, his bony knees cracking back into place.

"Will I see you again?" Asked Ben.

"Who knows? But be careful when you can, and decisive when you can't, Ben Hartley," and the Hermit shuffled past him, laying a dirty thin hand on his shoulder as he left. Ben felt like crying. He took out the orange scrap of cloth that he'd wrapped around Wolf's claw, and knew that the cloth would match one of the holes in the Hermit's t-shirt.

On the beach Wolf was sniffing at Ted and deciding whether to eat his ears or not. He decided against it. He smelled bad, rotten inside, and even Wolf had standards, although they were considerably lower than anyone else's. Then he changed his mind – his stomach was growling and complaining – and was about to take a bite from Ted's shoulder, but he noticed something about the wound in his chest. It was round, made by a musket ball. The same as in Richmond Park. So it had been the Hermit who had helped him during the Hunt. But why? What made a miserable bloke like him leave his hovel and put himself out to help them? He watched the Hermit shuffling like a raggedy bag of bones along the beach, and away. Wolf looked up. It was getting dark already, and there was a bad moon on the rise. In a few days it would be full, and Wolf thought that was when things would really get nasty.

Chapter Twenty

By the time they got back to Richmond Park it was quite dark, which was just as well because the whole place was an aftermath of carnage, the smell of blood and fear wet in the air. Some Sleepers were dead on the ground. One or two were wandering around dazed and bewildered, unable to sleep, unable to awaken. The grass was torn up and muddied where the chariots and Goatponies must have hurtled around catching their prey. It was a place where the birds would refuse to sing for a long time. The ground was scattered with belongings that no longer belonged, mementos of lives now destroyed: a gold ear ring, a child's teddy bear, a dog's chewed Frisbee, a mottled brown plastic comb, a hearing aid, a set of false teeth, a little notebook. Ben picked up the notebook and opened it. Inside were lists of things to do, names and addresses, then a message obviously scrawled in haste: *If anyone finds this, please tell my wife what I should have told her: that I love her more than life itself. What they are doing here in DreamTown is terrible – killing and hunting people.* There was a name and address in the inside front cover: JAMES MADISON, 124 COLEVILLE TERRACE, BRADFORD. Ben put the little notebook in his pocket.

Wolf sniffed the air.

"Lot of reapering gone down. Everyone got death slamming in their heads. You need big army of dreamtroopers to scuzz these bandits."

"And there's just me and you," said Ben.

Wolf chuckled, then spat and lit a cheroot.

"You only play the good odds, you ain't win nothing, chickadee. But time you was getting back. Morning soon and you bin here longtime. Dangerous you stay too long."

"Seems dangerous wherever I am. But why's it dangerous?"

"Stay too long you get caught in a comma," said Wolf.

"A comma. You mean like in punctuation?" asked Ben.

"Puncture-hating? Mebbe. But stuck in a comma. Then they's give you skug and all crapstuff in WakeTime and you get stuck in a comma. Your brain fried."

"Do you mean a coma? Like when you can't wake up?" Ben asked.

"Sure. Comma. Sleepdeath. So you gotta wake up. Get back, eat lots get your skullies nice n' stormed-up for the Harrowing," said Wolf.

"Afraid we can't allow him to go back," someone said, and before they could react one of the Hunters nets was fired and, like a giant spider's web, encircled Wolf and Ben and tightened. The rope bit into Ben's skin, his legs were yanked up and bent into his chest, his arms pinned to his sides. Wolf was coiled tight into a question mark, his long snout poking moistly into Ben's left eye. They were hauled up and thrown in a larger net, full of terrified life. The cart trundled out of the park. The voice had sounded familiar and as they passed under a streetlamp Ben saw the Mathematician standing watching them, his arms folded, a small smile on his lips. Looking more like Mr Braintree than ever he held one hand up and wiggled the fingers in a mocking goodbye gesture to Ben.

The cart rumbled on in the darkness. There were whimperings and cries and snuffles from the great squashed ball of people and animals caught in the net. Ben wondered if this was where it would all end. There was a part of him that would almost be relieved if it was over – the terrible ordeal of returning to DreamTown. He felt both old and young, a boy and a little old man. Mostly he felt plain exhausted. To feel tired when you were asleep was an odd thought and he tried to smile, though it was difficult with his face squashed against Wolf's. He wondered if they were all enemies – the Mathematician and Oswald, the Professor of Quantum

DreamPhysics, perhaps the Hermit too, although he somehow seemed outside of everything, and Ben thought he really had helped, almost as if he couldn't stop himself. And who was the figure on the beach playing the music? It could have been the Mathematician, but he was taller. Perhaps the Professor or, more likely, some horrible person Ben had yet to meet.

"What shall we do, Wolf?" Ben whispered.

Wolf tried to turn but his snout was now firmly lodged in Ben's left ear.

"We's keep still, 'til's I get my shnozz outta your lug," he whispered with difficulty. His fur was warm, though smelly.

"But you said I have to wake up soon," said Ben.

"Can't. Not in these catchers. They stop you wakeup."

So the nets stopped you from waking up. And then you stayed in DreamTown forever, if you survived. They trundled on for what seemed an age, then stopped outside some large metal gates. A shaven-headed man with a torch came and cast his light over the faces in the net, gave a brown-toothed grin, then opened the gates. The wagon wheeled in and stopped outside a huge warehouse. Dark and solid. A single light high up just below the roof illuminated a large sleeping face carved in grey stone. A face neither old nor young but in the grip of a terrible, agonising sleep that was strangling its features. Ben looked at it and a cold sweat dampened his forehead. The whole place had a feeling of death and long misery. A piston steamed and two metal doors began to part, brown vapour pouring out from within. The wagon was pulled inside and a metal claw came down from a crane, hooked the net, then lifted it high in the air, swung it around and lowered it into a large cage with thick mesh, so that neither people nor the smaller animals could escape. The net opened and they all tumbled out in a heap of limbs and fur and heads and claws. Two little twin boys, probably about eight, and alike as dots on a ladybird, clung to each other whimpering. Wolf stretched himself and yawned his jaw back into alignment. Then a gate clanged open and two little warriors with crossbows called to Ben and Wolf.

"You! Here!"

They were led out, across a dark oily path and into what appeared to be a large metal box. Inside there was a single bulb hanging from the ceiling. On one of the walls was a large screen. A barred gate clanged shut behind them, and a little warrior kept his crossbow trained on Wolf and Ben. Sitting on a wooden box was the Mathematician. He looked at Ben as if he was a complicated equation about to be solved once and for all.

Chapter Twenty One

"You're going to keep us here, aren't you? And I'll die 'cos I can't get back to my world, where my Mum is," said Ben.

"Not die exactly. Not like the others. But they'll think you're dead in WakeTime, then you are here for good. Metal is an excellent barrier. Prevents Sleepers returning, so this should do it," said the Mathematician, and he gave the metal wall of the box a bang with his fist. "It'll also stop you improvising your way out. That little Shakespeare might be good in his way, but metal just doesn't yield to it."

"I'm just a kid. I can't matter that much," said Ben.

The Mathematician smiled.

"You matter. More than you know. You're the one, but once you stay here you'll just be absorbed. Absorbed."

The word sounded horrible the way the Mathematician said it. He stretched it out – ab-sorbbedd … – so that it felt, to Ben, like a long rubbery mouth which would swallow him. Suddenly he knew that this is what the Mathematician had done to Mister Braintree – simply absorbed him.

The Mathematician glanced at Wolf, then back at Ben.

"And given that you two are so close, he might as well stay with you."

Wolf spat on the floor, then looked at the little armed Hunter who had his crossbow trained on him. He showed his teeth in something between a grin and a snarl.

"Yous and me, Shortpants, we's have our own reckoning. Soon. I grub you up whole, spit out yous little chicken-skinny bones for the dirtworms," he said, and spat again. The little Hunter licked his lips nervously, and Ben was scared that he might accidentally fire the bolt into Wolf.

"Mister Braintree, why are you doing this?" Ben asked.

For a moment the Mathematician's face changed. Momentarily he looked frightened and bewildered. His face seemed to crumble, fade, almost disappear, then it reassembled. *There is something else inside him.*

"There is no one by that name here," he said, but his eyes seemed to flicker with the ghost of a memory of someone else, of another time and place.

"What about all that work you was doing on dreams? All those Maths people working in that place that got bombed," said Ben.

"I keep them busy with futilities. It's all a distraction. This is the real work. Stopping you, then letting things take their course. One world absorbing another. There is a mathematical purity about two becoming one. "

"What about the one who plays that horrible flute sound? The one in the hood thing. Is he behind all this?"

"You'll meet him at the Harrowing, but by then it won't matter. You'll be a DreamTowner, with no card to play, no sword to wield, no numbers to play, as it were. Choose your own metaphor," said the Mathematician enigmatically.

The door opened and Professor Oswald Dawlish entered. He beamed at Ben.

"Excellent. Everything falls into place," then leaning forward conspiratorially, his bald dome gleaming like a pat of warm butter, "actually, now you're here for good, so to speak, I could tell you what the science is. All very interesting."

"Perhaps better to shut up for once, Oswald," said the Mathematician.

The little Professor shot a look of pure hatred at the Mathematician, then turned back to Ben.

"Do you know what beta waves are?" he asked.

Ben said he didn't, and noticed that Wolf lay down and closed his eyes, not remotely interested in anything the Professor had to say. He explained to Ben that Beta brain wave patterns are the most common and fastest brainwave pattern. It typically ranges from 14 Hertz to 32 Hertz and beyond.

Beta brainwaves are produced by your conscious mind during normal everyday thought process and waking consciousness. In sleep your beta patterns slow to between 0.5 and 8 Hertz. When people come to DreamTown during sleep Oswald and his team had found a way of keeping the beta levels down but at Focus Ten. What that means is that people know what is going on but are unable to wake up.

Oswald beamed proudly.

"Some die in the hunts and we just let some die anyway, because we don't need many survivors, but we'll keep a small force at Focus Ten. Once they are there it's permanent. We don't have to worry about locking them up. They stay in DreamTown forever."

"Like zombies. What do you want them for?" asked Ben.

"Human material is always useful. As workers, as an army should we need one, and for scientific research. The process is simple. Watch."

He took a remote from his pocket and switched on the monitor screen. The picture that came up made Ben's skin crawl.

Chapter Twenty Two

Even Wolf's eyes slide open and across to look at the picture on the screen. Those who had been in the net with them are now on a sort of conveyor belt, each one strapped into a chair which is on a moving belt that stops and starts, with a slight jolt. At the end of the line are two shaven headed Slammers and a Technician in a white coat. Now the Slammers fit a latticed mask over the head of each trapped prisoner so that all that is visible are the terrified eyes, a hole for the nose and another for the mouth. Now the Technician pulls a lever and a large needle comes down from above, piercing the skull, then a thick translucently grey fluid is sucked up into the glass hypodermic tube. When it is full, the needle is withdrawn. As the fluid enters there is a flinch, a momentary panic in the eyes, then a look of almost idiotic relinquishing, of pressure being released.

"You see, Ben. Relief in the eyes. No problems, no responsibilities, no decisions and regrets and uncertainties weighing them down. They are almost divorced from their own histories. Sometimes they have a sense of something past, like looking in a mirror and momentarily seeing someone else, but it's mercifully brief. It's a sort of freedom," said Oswald.

"You see the light go out in they's eyes. It's a kill," muttered Wolf.

"That part of the brain that could wake them up is no more. Gone. We don't bother with the animals and things. They just … get absorbed, and in any case we have our own creatures here, " said Oswald, with a derisive look at Wolf, and flicking the remote to show a large windowless room of mixed animals and birds all climbing over each other in a desperate pyramid to reach a tiny air vent in the ceiling. But all that came through it was the hiss of vapour, a cloud of yellow death, curling like a dragon's tongue with its message of death, and as panic set in they clawed and bit at each other, but it was all over very quickly.

Ben wanted to be sick; he wanted to scream. He felt his lungs tighten and reached for his inhaler but it was gone.

Swallow your scared, he thought and took deep breaths. Oswald was smiling at him. The Mathematician looked nervous; Wolf was looking at him as if he was a piece of prey.

"The glorious necessity of destruction, Ben Hartley," said Oswald, glowing beatifically. "Every seed is useless if it remains as it is, if it does not decay; because corruption always precedes generation. In this way Nature proceeds in all its operations, and when we want to imitate it, we must also blacken before whitening, destroy before regenerating, without which we will only produce rejects. Ha ha."

"You are seriously bonkers," said Ben. "Up the pole round the twist gone with the fairies stark bonkers."

"Oswald! Shut up. You've said more than enough," said the Mathematician who, since Ben called him Mister Braintree, seemed out of sorts.

"What about the explosion?"

Oswald looked at Ben with raised eyebrows.

"You know. What Einstein said. If DreamTown is anti-matter wotsit and WakeTime is matter, once they combine the whole lot could go up in a big bang," said Ben.

"Who told you that?" asked Oswald.

"He did," said Ben, looking at the Mathematician.

"You imbecile! Cretin!" snarled Oswald.

"I didn't tell him!" said the Mathematician.

"But what if it's true? You'll just be destroying everything," said Ben.

The two men looked at each other. They hated one another, but were chained together by dark knowledge.

"All science comes with a risk," said Oswald.

"A calculated risk. Einstein may be wrong, and my triumph will be to demonstrate it," said the Mathematician.

"*Our* triumph," corrected Oswald.

The Mathematician bowed in a flourish of sarcastic exaggeration to Oswald.

"Only you could have stopped it. And now we have you. Without you He will be free to start everything at the Harrowing," said Oswald.

"Who's he?" asked Ben.

But the question never got answered.

Chapter Twenty Three

They were interrupted by some scuffling outside, then the door opened and two little Hunters pushed in a pile of rags and bones, which wobbled to its feet and turned out to be the Hermit. He looked thinner and more ill than ever, and had a nasty cut on his cheek, and bruises on his bony arms.

"We found this piece of crap snooping outside," said one of the Little Hunters.

"What are you doing here? You look as if you've been in DreamTown long enough to know the South Side is for special work. It's a forbidden zone," said the Mathematician.

"I was curious. I saw the Hunt and I was curious. I wanted to know what happens afterwards," said the Hermit, looking from Wolf to Ben.

"You'll find out soon enough," said the Mathematician.

Minutes later the Mathematician and Oswald left, the door was bolted on the outside, and the three prisoners left for the night, watched by the Hunter with a crossbow, perched on a stool like a malevolent little goblin. His beetle-black eyes shone darkly. The Hermit sat down miserably. All three prisoners sat as far from the Hunter as they could and spoke in whispers.

"So much for my rescue mission," the Hermit said miserably.

"Hey, you helped us before," said Ben.

"More than one time, old Raggedy Man. You stink but you think," said Wolf, who then bit something irritating from his coat and swallowed it.

"But you have to get out of here, Ben. Get back, otherwise you're stuck here. Then the Harrowing will simply be a formality, because you'll be weak. Like me," added the Hermit, with a haunted look on his face.

"But I can't get back. I'm stuck. They said this metal will stop me waking up," said Ben miserably.

Ben and the Hermit continued to bemoan their imprisonment. When there was a pause Wolf spat on the floor.

"If you done whinging I can get you out," he said.

"How?" Ben and the Hermit asked at the same time.

"How you think I get to Waketime and back? Me a DreamTowner. My way. But it cost, chickadee. Ain't no chocolate party."

"But how will you take me too?" Ben asked.

"You hang on tight is all," then he looked at the Hermit. "Not you too, old gutsy. This ain't no slowtrain."

The Hermit gave a wan smile.

"I can't go back anyway. I'm a Longtimer here. And besides, it wouldn't be appropriate."

"But if you stay here ... that machine with the needle ..." said Ben, unable to finish.

"Take my chances," said the Hermit.

"Ok chickadee. But it's rush hour between DreamTown and WakeTime. Put something in your ears, otherhow the windrush scag up your jellymould. Hang on to me no matter what come our way. You see and hear the Universals rush and crush and skilter but you don't do nothing. You don't let unforeknowable events blood up your excitables otherwise you gone into the great Dark. The Long Goodbye where it's always a bad moon on the rise. Just hang on your skoolies whatever. You skif me?"

Ben nodded, and tore up a snotty tissue and stuffed it in his ears. His Mum would be appalled, but that was hardly a problem right now.

"Suppose it don't work," said Ben. "I mean, you've done it before but alone. With me it might be too hard."

"Everything too hard if you think about it, chickadee," said Wolf.

"Besides, you already have the experience of being in two places at once, so think of it as something you can easily achieve," said the Hermit.

Ben looked at him. What did he mean? The Hermit smiled.

"You're here, aren't you? And it's all frighteningly real. I thought that by coming here I could escape the Real, but you never can. It makes a visitation upon you. So you're here, but you are also tucked up in bed in WakeTime, dreaming. If someone went in your bedroom you would be there. See? You are in two places at once. If you can achieve that you can go on this Rushour journey" He smiled, a light in his eyes, so that despite the dirt-ingrained wrinkles, scuzzy beard, bad teeth and smell almost as questionable as Wolf's, he really did seem like a figure of joyful wisdom. Briefly.

"Time to fly," said Wolf.

Ben held Wolf tight around the neck. The sinewy muscle beneath the thick fur was lean and taut. Wolf's eyes slid redly to one side, then closed, and he raised his muzzle slowly. At first it was a stillness, a breath that held them all, then a note so low Ben felt the vibration before he heard the sound, a moan that carried all the pain of this and any other world. It rose in pitch and gained in volume. The moan became a call – to whom? To what thing out there in the dark? Wolf's eyes were still closed, his muzzle pointing straight up at the ceiling, his shoulders taut and his neck like a fluted chamber, from which the howl now grows and swells and rises and heightens until it seems everything will break and splinter. Ben smells landscapes, great pine trees in the snow, vistas of mountains and valleys and forests so ancient they collapse back into themselves and grow again. There is rain and wind and bleak morning sun, the clip of long nails on ice, the safety of the pack, the beauty of the kill and the danger of everything. He wants to ask where Wolf is taking him, but he knows the answer – everywhere.

AAAAAAAOOOOOOWWWWWW... and on it goes, so loud now that everything else is ghostly and thin. Ben is dimly aware of the Hunter shouting and pointing his crossbow at Wolf, of the Hermit grasping the Hunter around the neck and dragging him to the floor, but all this is a thousand miles away. There is only Wolf, Ben, and the Howl that seems to stretch into everything that ever was, as strong as a rock and as tender as an eye, and it is as if they are turning, like a column of air, riding and pivoting on the howl from which there is no escape. You can only follow it. And that is exactly what they did, out into the night, into the strangeness and turmoil of Rushhour, when dreams are at their busiest, their most dense, and certainly their most frightening.

Chapter Twenty Four

At first they move slowly through a tunnel, like the underground tube, while everything rushes at them. It is like being in a crowd when everyone else is going the opposite way to you. Dreams flash by, some shaped like bubbles, others like balloons, some like raggedy bags with holes, with dream fragments dripping out – leaking dreams; some like large transparent faces. Dreams of escape, of persecution, torment, rage and frustration, and some gentler elysian dreams of oceans with unheard of colourful fish, forests with bears and lions and deer, great crashing cities that sway with the breath of the dreamer. And people, endless people, a great army of sleep refugees, some like ordinary people, others more ghostly, shadows of their waking selves, but Ben thinks of the Hunt, of the nets, the bodies, of the terrible factory of removal where people lose their identities. How many of these souls will return?

Wolf is exhausted. The effort of moving against the tide of dreams is painful, and Ben feels Wolf's muscles tighten, his breathing rasp, but instead of resting or slowing down, he seems determined to go faster, to keep a momentum, whatever the cost. The tunnel widens as more dreams come at them, some floating amiably Howdoyoudo-diddly-oo?, some crashing like waves, some in an angry red mist and one or two hurtling at them like missiles, but dispersing at the last moment and reforming after passing around them. Now Wolf is panting as he struggles on, and Ben tightens his grip on his neck as the dreams threaten to pull him away – then he would be lost, drowned in a tide of dreams gushing back to DreamTown.

"Chickadee, loosen up. You strangulerating my tubes!" chokes Wolf, and Ben loosens his grip a little, but still holds firm to the loose fur at his throat.

Ben is horrified to see a smaller, wispier version of his Mum, encased in what looks like a transparent Easter egg, and all around her inside are little angry red tails, like currents of electricity, snapping and curling and straightening. Like worms, he thinks: *I have to get back and wake her up, otherwise she might get caught in the Hunt.* He is aware of sounds, the tunnel full of whispers and sniggers and cries half heard, then gone, like voices in the wind. Ben knows that Wolf is running on pure will power, his strength nearly gone. He feels Wolf's back legs buckle, but with an immense effort and a grunt he steadies and keeps going.

Ben thinks: *This is too much. Alone, he could do it, but with me hanging on, it's too much. I've destroyed him as well as myself. Everything's my fault.* As if in reply, there is a great bursting through; with a gasp from Ben and a grunt from Wolf they tumble onto his bedroom floor.

Wolf lay there panting for a minute or so, white foam flecking his chops and whiskers, his mouth pulled back in a grimace, eyes half closed, chest heaving. Ben looked around at the strange familiarity of his room in the dark, but with Wolf there, a confusion of worlds. Ben felt exhausted, his throat dry as a bone, his head pounding, his mind still full of the myriad rush of dreams. He ran to check on his Mum. She was there, asleep. He'd wake her up in a minute, just to make sure her dream didn't keep her there. He crept to the kitchen and drank a long glass of cool water, then took Scrap's dish of water back to Wolf, which he slurped up, then lay down again, panting.

"I gotta shuteye longtime, chickadee, but somewhere safe. No one see me," he said.

"Under my bed," said Ben, and Wolf crept under Ben's bed, into a chaos of dirty socks, underwear, shirts, sweet wrappers and fluff balls. Within minutes he was snoring. Ben thought his Mum might hear, so he put a few sweaters and his dressing gown on the floor to muffle the sound. But where was Scrap? He should have been on Ben's bed, on his back with his feet in the air, his nose twitching with rabbity-chasing dreams. He would be terrified of Wolf, so he'd probably scarpered and was hiding, trembling, behind the sofa. *I'll check in a minute*, Ben thought as he crept into his Mum's room.

"Mum. Mum!"

She woke up, the look in her eyes suggesting she was still half in DreamTown.

"Ben. I was having such a strange dream,"

"I know," said Ben.

She looked at him as if he had a boil on the end of his nose. He had an urge to tell her everything, just howl like a child and tell her. Let her take over. Relinquish all responsibility. Even as he had the thought, he knew he wouldn't do it. He was bound on a wheel and had to turn with it. Right now he needed some sleep, then a day where he could take it easy, let Wolf sleep without being discovered, then go back to DreamTown for whatever new crisis waited.

"It's nearly light," his Mum said. "I'll get up soon. You go back to bed, love."

He kissed her on the cheek and went to the living room and looked behind the sofa, expecting to see Scrap's bright, alarmed eyes, then to get covered in wet doggy kisses. Nothing. He looked under chairs, the table, behind the cooker in the kitchen. Nothing. Then he noticed the door. It was a shade open. His Mum must have left it open and Scrap got through. He ran out into the garden. Morning light freshly revealed everything and a few birds were twittering, but there was no Scrap.

"Scrap! Scrap boy! Here!"

Nothing. No gleeful run. No panting. No joy. Where was he? And how long had he been gone? Perhaps only a short while, if he heard or smelled Wolf and got frightened. Why did everything go wrong at once? He hadn't asked for any of this. Sitting on a pile of bricks a large tear welled and dripped muddily down his cheek. The garden looked misty and he saw that the little scrubby lawn was laced with a filigree of dew-laden spider webs, catching the light like a tapestry of diamonds. The sun started its diurnal warming and he felt something in his pocket. He almost jumped, thinking it might be an insect, but when he reached in, a sleepy little face opened its sticky eyes and yawned so hugely the little hamster's jaw almost cracked.

Chapter Twenty Five

"But where did you get him?" Mrs Hartley asked, as Ben put the little albino hamster on the kitchen table, where he stood on his hind legs and washed his whiskers and ears, then sniffed the air and headed for Ben's crunchy nut cornflakes. He was hungry after his epic sleep and journey from DreamTown and Ben put a few flakes on the table. The little hamster picked one up and started to eat it like a squirrel eating a nut.

Ben could have said to his Mum: "I rescued him on a beach from committing suicide and from a bunch of marauding zombies led by Ted who was then killed by a mad old smelly hermit." Somehow, this didn't seem a good idea, unless Ben wanted to go back to the nuthouse clinic.

"He just sort of appeared in my pocket," said Ben.

"What's his name?" asked Mrs Hartley.

"Mushroom," said Ben.

Mushroom suddenly stopped eating the flake and fell instantly asleep. Ben looked alarmed. He picked up Mushroom and the little creature awoke with a yawn. Ben was worried he'd slip back to DreamTown, perhaps on the dreaded beach again.

"He's got narcolepsy," said Mrs Hartley.

"What's that?" asked Ben. His Mum didn't usually use long words.

"Means you keep nodding off."

She had a strange wistful look on her face.

"Your Dad used to like dictionaries. Got on better with 'em than he did people. I remember him saying once that Narcolepsy'd be a good thing, 'cos when everything got too much you could just drop off, like a little holiday from reality. He had lots of ideas like that. Maybe that's why you go a bit funny sometimes. Got it from him."

"Thanks," said Ben, but his sarcasm was lost on his Mum. She was looking at the back door.

"It's not like Scrappy to go running off. He's too ... cowardly," she said. "I'll ring the police, and the Canine Defence League, see if he's been found. He's not been right since you went all funny."

"I'll go and look for him," said Ben, not wishing to continue this conversation.

He found an old bird cage in the cellar, cleaned it up, put some bits of wool and paper in and let Mushroom in. Immediately the little hamster got busy and started building a nest for himself, with frequent sleeps that sometimes only lasted a few seconds. There was also the problem of Wolf, asleep under his bed. It would be a disaster if his Mum found him. He went into his room and spent a few minutes making it even more untidy, scattering clothes and books and games all over the floor. He had to hope that if his Mum came in she would take one look at the disgusting mess and go out again.

Ben re-traced the paths of thousands of walks he had done with Scrap over the years. He shouted his name and looked with dread into the river where Scrap would sometimes take a dip. If his dog had drowned he wasn't sure he'd have the strength to go back to DreamTown and face whatever was awaiting him. He went to Jack's old house to see if Scrap had taken refuge there, but although Max and Bobby were delighted to see Ben, there was no Scrap. Where was he? Perhaps someone had dognapped him and would hold him to ransom, but even Ben had to admit, fiercely as he loved his little friend and confidant, that if someone was going to steal a valuable dog, Scrap would be pretty low on the list. Maybe even last.

While Ben was looking anxiously and increasingly despondently for Scrap a newspaper headline caught his eye as he passed a shop: SLEEPDEATH – THE NEW PLAGUE? He stopped and read the first paragraph of the article:

Doctors are concerned about a recent increase in the number of people dying in their sleep, for no apparent reason. Worryingly, it appears to be happening the world over. Some medical authorities speculate that there must be a new virus causing the deaths, but as yet no one can identify it. The Daily Trumpet asks the question no one else dare ask: Is this a Terrorist plot to destroy our world? (See p.4 for the Editor's opinion)

He picked up another paper which had a photograph of the Prime Minister in the Houses of Parliament, his head resting on the dispatch box, eyes closed and a slight dribble from his mouth, as if a snail had recently crawled out. All around him MPs were asleep, heads on chests, or slumped forwards or sideways. The Foreign Minster's head was resting against the head of the Minister for Home Affairs, both of whom were sworn enemies and hated the sight of each other. Now they were sleeping like Siamese twins. WHEN WILL OUR GOVERNMENT WAKE UP? asked the headline. The report started: "Cleaner at Westminster Daisy Sharp told our Reporter: 'They all just dropped off. The silence is wonderful.'"

A loud KERASH made Ben start and turn around. There was a searing and grinding and scraping of metal that made his teeth hurt. A bus had ploughed into a lamp post, which was jutting out from beneath it like a strange rhinoceros horn at an angle. People on the bus were shouting and screaming. Ben ran over to help. A man was forcing open the emergency door with a spanner he'd got from his car. Everyone inside looked terrified, but no one seemed seriously hurt. It was difficult to work out what had happened as there were no other vehicles involved. Ben ran to the front of the bus and the driver was slumped sideways.

"Heart attack," said a woman behind him, but Ben knew better. The driver was asleep, snoring soundly, and probably in the long tunnel to DreamTown, from which he may not return.

It's close, thought Ben. *Whatever it is, it's close.*

And tonight is full moon.

Chapter Twenty Six

Ben's Mum was finding it difficult to get going. She felt so tired. It wasn't like her and she thought she might be coming down with a cold. Having made a strong cup of instant coffee with three sugars, she went into the garden to look for Scrap. Where could he have gone? He was such a scaredy-cat dog that wherever he was he must be so frightened. She sighed, went indoors and decided to make Ben's bed. She opened the door and stopped dead. The room was a complete tip. It looked as it had been ransacked by a demented bear. And then – there was the smell. This wasn't just socks, or Scrap, or unwashed boy. This was something else? Mrs Hartley sniffed and gulped down a wave of nausea as she was met by a noxious pot pourri that might have been designed by a perfumier whose job was to create the most disgusting, ineffable, revolting, breath-stopping pong imaginable. Meat and damp leaves and mud and cigar smoke and something else she preferred not to think about.

It seemed to be coming from under the bed. Mrs Hartley bent down but all she could see was a raggedy pile of dirty clothes. She was going to rummage around but decided it was pointless and the best thing to do would be go to the shops since it was her morning off and buy several bottles of the strongest disinfectant she could find, have a nip of brandy, peg her nose, then attack Ben's room as if it was a war zone.

Mrs Hartley sensed rather than saw that the outside world was different. The air seemed heavy and depressed, as if a curtain was over everything and nothing could breathe properly. There were too few people about. She stopped suddenly when an old lady at a bus stop stepped in front of her and gazed up, pointing her bony, liver-spotted hand, fingers like church spires, at something behind. A window cleaner was at the top of a ladder leaning against a block of flats. Three storeys up, he had slumped against the ladder, either unconscious or *surely he can't be asleep* and the ladder was starting to slide sideways against the wall.

"No! No!" shouted Mrs Hartley, but it was too late.

The ladder slid a little more and the man fell soundlessly from it, completely relaxed like a doll, asleep. The second and a half it took him to reach the ground seemed like years. Then a *whumpf* as all the air was knocked from his body, and he bounced a metre back in the air then crashed down again. It was obvious from the angle of his head that he would not be cleaning any more windows. Mrs Hartley felt a sob in her throat. The wide-eyed old lady with her could do nothing but point, her finger trembling.

When Ben returned he half hoped Scrap would be there at the front door, wriggling in ecstatic circles and wagging his tail furiously, then rolling over to have his tummy tickled. His Mum was out, perhaps looking for Scrap. Ben checked under the bed, and Wolf was still asleep. Today was meant to be for resting and having a good meal, so that he'd be ready to go back to DreamTown for the 'Harrowing', whatever that was, but it hadn't turned out like that. The world was going seriously awry. Ben felt exhausted, but knew he wouldn't sleep. So he decided to have one more hunt for Scrap. As she was out he started in his Mum's room. He looked behind the wardrobe, then under the bed. There was an old cardboard shoe box which he pulled out and looked inside. There were photographs of him when he was a baby, his Mum holding him and smiling, looking younger and more hopeful than she ever looked now. Then there was a photograph of a clean shaven man staring fiercely at the camera. On the back it just said Tom. So that was his Dad. Why had she never shown him this photograph before? Why had he never asked? He looked through the box for more photographs of his Dad, but this was the only one. *It's him it's him you know it's him.*

Holding the photograph up to the light from the window, he felt something grow in his stomach, rise up, like a live thing desperate to get out. It's him. He knew it was from the eyes: haunted and looking at what might be beyond, always beyond. Add more than ten years, a lot of hard living, dirt, whiskers and straggly hair. It was him. The Hermit. His Dad was the Hermit in DreamTown. And he knew Ben was his son. He must do. That's why he reacted to his name. That's why he'd been following Ben and helping him. But why didn't he tell him? Ben felt a mixture of anger and longing to see him again. It was his Dad.

Chapter Twenty Seven

Mrs Hartley poured a generous amount of brandy in her tea and sat sipping it, wondering what on earth was going on. She almost choked when she saw the photograph of Tom, her long gone husband, on the table. Ben was in the doorway, staring reproachfully.

"You said you didn't have any photos of my Dad," he said.

"I forgot," said Mrs Hartley, instantly regretting the lie. "I mean, not exactly forgot, more ... it seemed for the best. You know. He was gone. He wasn't coming back. He was lost somehow."

"He's my Dad. I could have at least known what he looked like."

"I loved him very much. I think he loved me, in his own demented sort of way." Mrs Hartley blinked, tears welled, and she took a large sip of brandy-tea.

"I know where he is," said Ben. There was no point in pretending any more.

Mrs Hartley stared at him. She put another dollop of brandy in her tea, put down the mug and swigged straight from the brandy bottle.

"Ben, don't go all funny again. I can't afford the taxi to that ... hospital. And you haven't got any clean pants."

"Really. I know where he is. He looks different. Older. A bit of a mess really. But he tried to help me, us, and I'd love to see him again," said Ben, and his shoulders slumped as two big tears coursed down leaving muddy rivers on his cheeks.

Mrs Hartley opened her arms and Ben came to her. They hugged for a minute.

"I don't know why everything's so hard, love. Where did you see him?"

Ben wondered how he could possibly explain. It involved so much and his Mum wouldn't believe it and she'd have him taken back to the Funny Farm and he'd miss the Harrowing and everything would be a bigger mess than it already was, if that was possible. Instead, he didn't have to say a word, because Wolf did.

"Little chickadee seed Old Hermit back in my chock o' the woods, lady," said Wolf, who seemed to fill the doorway of Ben's bedroom.

Mrs Hartley's jaw dropped open into a perfect O. Her eyes widened in horror and her nose wrinkled in revulsion.

"Ben, there's a ... a ... wotsit, a big hairy, smelly, talking killing thing ... quick. Run!"

"It's all right, Mum. He's my friend. He saved my life. Several times actually."

Mrs Hartley sat down heavily, unable to take her eyes off Wolf. There was something shadowy about him, like a figure from a dream, even though the smells were overpoweringly real.

"Honest. He's dead good at ... protecting me and stuff," said Ben.

"Yeah yeah, Hip hooray for me," said Wolf, hawking and spitting something green on the carpet. "I's regular heroical. More to the point, chickadee, I's gut grumbling. We need grog up before the long backbreak to DreamTown. You got any grubmeat? A skizzbat or a lubjumper. Live or dead anyways it skugs."

Mrs Hartley stared at Wolf uncomprehendingly.

"Your maternal look brainpoled, chickadee. How's about you check out the dead box?"

"I think he means the fridge," said Ben, and opened the door.

"What do you want?" He asked.

"Everything," said Wolf.

Mrs Hartley watched in shock as Ben took out a lump of cheese, some sausages, half a chicken she'd meant to throw away, a dish of cold custard, a frozen beef curry and a mouldy lettuce. He put them all on the floor. Wolf sneered at the lettuce, spat on it, then devoured everything else in thirty seconds flat. He licked his lips, gave a meaty belch, then flicked a spark from a claw and lit a cheroot.

"There's no smoking in here," said Mrs Hartley, desperate to cling on to some normal rules.

"Then go some elseplace, Mrs Woman," said Wolf with a smile, and his eyes slid from gold to red. Then suddenly his ears pricked and he looked towards the door.

"Check the sky, chickadee. Itsa coming," he said.

Ben opened the kitchen door and looked outside. It was growing dark and there, hung low and ominous in the sky like a warrior's bloody shield was the biggest moon he'd ever seen. *This is it*, he thought. *The bad moon* is here. Mrs Hartley looked at it too and felt a chill in her heart.

"I think they call it a harvest moon," she said.

Wolf wheezed a chuckle.

"The harvest be you tonight, Mrs Woman. We don't get back everyone be reapered."

"Ben, come in the living room please," said Mrs Hartley.

Leaving Wolf to enjoy his smoke, they went next door and Ben spent fifteen fruitless minutes trying to explain about DreamTown. The more he said the less likely it seemed. The one undeniable fact in his favour was that there was a talking, chuckling, smoking, smelly thing that might be a wolf, and that was unbelievable, but there he was in their flat, so perhaps his Mum might believe the rest.

She didn't. Eventually she agreed not to do anything until the morning. Secretly she was hoping that Wolf might be an illusion. She'd had a scare with the window cleaner, she'd also had a lot of brandy and felt churned up talking about Ben's dad, and all that strange nonsense about him living as a hermit in somewhere called DreamTown. It was all too much.

Perhaps in the morning it would all seem like a bad dream. So eventually she went to bed clutching the brandy bottle.

"When will we leave?" asked Ben

"Soon as you hit long gone shuteye and step into the dark. I be there and we journey," said Wolf.

Before going to bed Ben went to check on his new little friend, Mushroom. The little hamster was fast asleep, and Ben was just about to leave when he stopped and gaped. There, scratched in the sawdust at the bottom of the cage, was a message. Ben rubbed his eyes, but the message was still there, in wobbly letters:

How are my Bobby and Max?

It didn't make sense. How could a little hamster know Bobby and Max? And what did the 'my' mean. Only Jack would say that and Jack was ...

"Jack?" Ben asked, peering into the cage.

The little hamster stirred in his sleep, then gave another jaw-breaking yawn and opened his eyes and blinked. He looked at Ben and went very still, only his whiskers twitching, and Ben knew.

"They're fine, though they miss you. They always will. But Max and Bobby are all right, Jack."

Ben put his finger against the cage and the hamster came up and brushed it with his whiskers, then curled up again in the little nest he'd made himself and went back to sleep. Was this really some sort of reincarnated Jack, or was the little hamster a messenger for wherever or whatever Jack now was?

It was too weird to think about.

Chapter Twenty Eight

Ben found it impossible to get to sleep. Wolf lay on the floor, alert, occasionally looking at the full, bright, reddish moon through the bedroom window. It seemed a living thing of blood and foreboding. Where was Scrap? What would the Harrowing be? And his Dad … it didn't bear thinking about. Ben tried to calm his thoughts and remember some of what he'd been told. *Imaginary numbers are like shadows – they tell you something about the real world. If matter and anti-matter meet, it might be the end of everything. We are such stuff as dreams …* these things might be important to remember in whatever was about to happen. What else? *Swallow your scared.* Ben rubbed the pentagram mark on his arm and Wolf immediately turned, his ears upright and fur almost crackling. His eyes glowed reddish gold, like the moon, but stronger. The eyes were a weight, pressing Ben down into the great darkness, a letting go of the world. Ben's own eyes flickered, closed, flickered again, then shut tight. Sleep came like a sudden fog.

It was easier getting back. They could ride the great wash of dreams tumbling and swirling to DreamTown. Ben hung on to his back as Wolf leapt and darted and balanced his way through the Tunnel, like a dancer riding logs on a helter skelter river. Ben almost enjoyed it. He'd forgotten what it was just to have fun, although this ride could be taking them to the end of everything.

With a great bursting through and a whoosh of air they tumbled out and rolypolled on a grassy hill in the darkness. Wolf lay down to recover, panting heavily. Ben rubbed his back where he'd fallen and looked up. The moon had grown redder and he was sure he could see a crack that resembled a crooked, malevolent smile. *Bad moon now risen. And what now?* Wolf stood and Ben noticed that one back leg trembled slightly. This journey back and forth had taken its toll. Before, he'd thought Wolf practically invincible, now he saw his Guide and friend was deeply tired. As if he'd read Ben's thoughts Wolf's eyes narrowed redly and he spat on the ground. "I's best when there's bad odds, chickadee. Get skullied up and mean in the bones. Little chavvo like you no worry – this your big night, billy'o. Stand strong and ready for whatever scugs out the Great Dark." He flipped a cheroot between his teeth, sparked a claw, settled down to smoke and wait. His ears suddenly pricked. Something was happening.

Three hundred metres away a blazing trail of figures snaked its way uphill. Men, women, children, animals. Nomads flanked the procession, lighting the way with flaming torches. Everyone was humming – a low drone of expectation and inevitability. They just kept coming – hundreds, thousands. Ben could now see they were going to a huge building on the top of a hill. Floodlights made it stand out against the night like a giant wedding cake.

"This the Allypally," said Wolf. "The Harrowing."

"What do we do?" Ben asked.

"Go look it in the eye," said Wolf.

He loped off in the semi darkness, keeping his distance from the procession. Ben followed. He took a quick blast from his asthma inhaler and tried to keep calm. *Swallow your scared.* After a few hundred metres, they crossed a road in shadow, went up some steps and Wolf loped to the back of the building. The crowds were so dense it was easy to get through unnoticed, although Ben kept his head down and Wolf moved so silently and swiftly that people felt a brush against their legs, a whiff of strangeness, but by then he had gone. The building was almost full but the crowds kept coming and were congregating outside. Speakers and huge plasma screens were being erected so they could see inside. The main hall was being shown on the screens, packed to capacity, some people standing on window ledges, and a few monkeys hanging from drapes. At the far end of the hall was a stage with bright red drapes hanging down to the floor. The drapes had markings on them but Ben couldn't make them out. There was a great sense of festival and apocalypse. Something that would change things forever.

Wolf suddenly stopped near the back entrance and made a sharp turn away. Ben looked inside and saw something that chilled his blood and made him gasp.

Chapter Twenty Nine

Just inside, guarding the inner door to the Great Hall and stairways, were some of the most unhinged creatures Ben had ever seen. About six feet tall, wearing bright green jackets, long arms like apes but with great reptilian claws for hands that shone like polished chrome. Bizarrely, three legs sporting Doc Marten boots. Their heads were large oval shapes with yellowish, short cropped blond hair, wide slits of mouths that seemed to be constantly whispering some private mantra. The eyes were shocking. A blink away from madness. They flickered stories of disorder, confusion, and a great violence.

"Deliriums," said Wolf, as he and Ben hid in the shadows by a wall of Allypally. "Them's the worst. Gob away from the great barking chaotical. Them's choke the spit from you. Gibber your spine out like a fish flip. Strong as the Reaper's knife."

Wolf told Ben he had to be close to things in the Great Hall, but that the Deliriums and everyone else would try to capture him. They had to find a way to get in the Great Hall without being seen. They shadowed the outside wall and then Wolf stopped. A builder's ladder lay abandoned. Ben leaned it against the wall, and Wolf somehow managed to coil his body and climb the ladder, Ben following and trying not to look down. Near the end of the ladder, fifteen metres up, was a rusted window. Wolf curled his paws around it and tried to lever it open. Stuck fast. The ladder wobbled precariously as Ben joined him and helped to force the latch. Finally it groaned and with a spray of fine rust opened a few inches. Wolf put his front paws in and forced it open, then scrambled inside, followed by Ben. It was dark with a smell of dust and damp. They climbed up a narrow flight of stairs. Then another, and another, until there were no more. Ben opened a tiny hatch door in the wall and looked inside. They were just beneath the giant roof, and wooden beams stretched out into the darkness. Wolf stepped onto one and looked back at Ben.

"You stays on the wood, chickadee, otherwise you drop through the ceiling like a skugbat in a downwind."

It was dark and smelly, and it took all Ben's energy to cling to the rafters as they made their way along the roof. The gap between roof and joists was little more than a metre, so Ben could only stoop. He tried to close his mind against spiders and creeping things in the dark. After ten minutes a boom boom and a humming and hissing like the whisper of dry leaves told them they were above the Great Hall. There were cracks and tiny holes and Ben could see the Hall way way below, the crowd getting more and more excited. For a second Ben imagined falling through the thin plaster and the terrible certain knowledge of death as he swirled a hundred and fifty metres down. As if knowing his thoughts, Wolf hissed.

"Keep your headjelly on tight, Chickadee. This not weaktime. Strong for whateveritis."

They perched on a slim wooden joist and looked through a tiny hole in the plaster ceiling down at the crowd, the faded glory of great drapes and velvet curtains, an air of anticipation. Suddenly there was silence. Lights dimmed. A drumbeat began, then grew faster and faster, until everyone in the Hall was stamping and flapping and shouting. Six Deliriums carved a way through the crowd and stood onstage, then from behind the stage a hooded figure appeared to tumultuous applause and approached a lectern to stand on a box. It was the same figure they had seen that awful day of the suicides on the beach. When it held up its arms to thundering shouts and applause, it was like being at a football match when the winning goal is scored. Then the arms dropped and everyone was silenced.

Ben tried to look at the figure's face, but it was shadowed by the hood.

"The Harrowing," said the Figure, and the silence became a subdued chill. "The night we've all waited for. Bad Moon. Blood Moon. You Longtimers have all done so well. Now you get your rewards. Tonight no one returns to Waketime. It's over. Tonight Waketime ceases to be. There will only be DreamTown."

A shouting and waving and cheering began, then subsided.

"Many who arrive tonight will be absorbed. Some will become builders, carpenters, cooks – and who will be their Masters? You!"

The Figure held out his arms to embrace them all, and there was wild cheering. DreamTown would be a place of slaves and masters, and this was the party to celebrate the masters. Oswald and the Professor came and joined the Hooded figure, but Ben thought they looked uneasy rather than jubilant and victorious. Then he heard a rafter creak behind him and knew without looking that they'd been fooled. They had walked right into a trap. He turned and shivered at what he saw.

Chapter Thirty

There, crouched in the shadows, were two Deliriums, one grinning at Ben and Wolf and the other watchful, menacing, with a long scar that ran down his broad forehead, across one eye and down his cheek. Just looking at their eyes made Ben want to wet himself. Windows into chaos and insanity. *Swallow your scared.* Wolf put his head on his front paws and just looked at the two huge creatures. Then he yawned. Ben thought this was the coolest thing he had ever seen. Or perhaps the silliest. The grinning Delirium's mouth started to twitch.

"You two threelegs gonna just sit there like dropturds all night, or you wanna get busy with something?" said Wolf, and spat into the darkness.

"It finishes here. You finish here," said Scarface. "And once we squeeze the juice from you, Ben Hartley, nothing stops the Harrowing."

The grinning Delirium switched on a torch and shone it at Ben.

"I wanna see his eyes pop when he goes," he said, and giggled, curiously high pitched for such a large creature. He shifted his weight from two of his legs to the third, and balanced, ready to spring at Ben.

If this is it, I'm not going to be a coward, not in front of Wolf, thought Ben. And he felt calm, able to think. Imaginary numbers. Little Shakespeare and his head teeming with words. Such words. It was as if a gate were opening in Ben's head. *Language is a weapon too.* Ben looked down at the hooded Figure, then back at the Deliriums.

"His promises were, as he then was, mighty; But his performance, as he is now, nothing."

What does this mean?

As if answering his own question, Ben said: "I think it means he's fooling you."

The two Deliriums looked at each other.

"Once it's over. The Harrowing. Once Waketime is absorbed, gone forever, what do you think will happen? He won't need you any more," said Ben.

"He thinks we're stupid. Close your ears. It's a lie," said Scarface to Grinner.

"What do you do? Kill, guard, control, stuff like that. He won't need you. Wouldn't be surprised if he takes you to that factory on the south side. The needle in the head. You'll be a drooling bag of fat," said Ben, not knowing where any of this was coming from, but feeling he was getting through. They wouldn't believe him, but it was buying time.

More words swam into his head. And what else had little Shakespeare said? *Improvise. Improvise.*

"Shake off this downy sleep, death's counterfeit, and look on death itself!"

And he raised his arms as Wolf struck a flinty spark with a claw and it seemed momentarily there was something there, in the flickering half light, a suggestion of living darkness, come to claim what was due. The grinning Delirium was staring at Ben's raised arm. Ben realised it was the pentagram mark that had captivated him and he moved his arm closer to the Delirium, and the creature seemed hypnotised. It all happened in a moment, but a moment was enough for Wolf to spring. He went straight for the throat and got a good grip, but the Delirium was strong and his metal claw-like hands gripped the back of Wolf's head and dug deep in the flesh, trying to pull his head away. Ben could only watch, catching glimpses of the fight from the torchlight that had fallen on a rafter. The other Delirium was somewhere in the shadows, waiting. There was barely room for a fight, and Wolf and the Delirium seemed locked into each other in the dark, dust swirling everywhere. Ben saw Wolf's red eye close in pain as the Delirium tore an ear almost completely off. A thin jet of blood arced from the Delirium's throat and over Ben's arm. A howl as something snapped, wood breaking, bone and sinew and muscle tearing from each other. The two spun over and Wolf got a fresh grip on the Delirium's face. A searing scream that Ben would remember forever as an eye was torn out. With a violent last effort the Delirium got Wolf in a bear hug and spun himself over. The two figures crashed against the roof, then down onto the thin plaster of the ceiling.

"Noooo!" screamed Ben as the conjoined creatures, as if in a deadly embrace, smashed through the ceiling and fell, turning and twirling, Wolf still with battle in his eyes and biting deep into the Delirium's shoulder. As they fell and twisted and turned Ben said aloud: "Let Wolf land on top." And as if someone or something had heard at the last second the Delirium flipped over and hit the floor like a living bomb, Wolf on top, his fall partially broken. The Delirium gasped as the air was pushed from him, as his head smashed on the Hall floor. Wolf was up, snarling, one ear almost gone, one leg smashed beyond repair, cuts all along his back, his mouth like a bloody gash, but ready to take on everyone and everything if he had to. Ben choked and almost wanted to fall through the hole, just to be with Wolf.

Shock rippled through the Great hall, then stilled. Everyone had backed away, and Wolf was now in a little space, surrounded by thousands, the dead Delirium by him. Wolf snarled and dared anyone to come for him. Six Nomads and four Deliriums closed in at a signal from the Hooded Figure on the stage. The Nomads had pointed sticks and hatchets. The Deliriums had their claws. Ben opened his mouth to scream at them, to do something to save his beloved Guide, but no sound came. An icy cold metallic claw closed over his mouth, and another held him tightly around the chest.

Chapter Thirty One

Ben was led through the crowd, which parted like sand to make way, and everyone gawped at him. The Delirium held him tightly by the arm. Ben looked around for Wolf – there was blood and fur on the ground, and at least two dead Nomads being carted away. Even half dead, Wolf must have put up a hell of a fight. Where was he now? Carved into bits? Thrown outside for the crows? Burnt as rubbish? Tears pricked Ben's eyes but he swallowed them back. Wolf never felt self pity, and what was Ben feeling now except his own loss? Defeat weighed on him, but this had to be seen through. Wolf had given his life for it, so Ben had to do all he could to stop the takeover of Waketime.

The Delirium pulled Ben to a halt. He looked up at the stage and the Hooded Figure looked down, the Mathematician and Oswald flanking him. Ben could feel the Figure's eyes on him, although he couldn't see them. They seemed to be lulling him into a kind of sleep, but he was already asleep. Wasn't he?

"Ben Hartley. You and Wolf have caused us considerable trouble, but it's over now. In a few hours there will be only DreamTown. Look! "

On a great screen behind him a light flashed and, suddenly, there was the tunnel, with thousands and thousands of dreaming people and animals and birds coming to DreamTown, to their living death. Ben felt overwhelmed by it all. Maybe it was better that way. Maybe it was just easier to let everything happen. The eyes were still on him. He was so weary. He looked down. There was a spot of blood and a tuft of fur. Shame flooded him. He had to make an effort, whatever the cost. The pentagram mark on his arm throbbed. Then he got help from an unlikely source.

The Hooded Figure lifted up his arms and the crowd looked at him expectantly, but Ben suddenly understood. He jumped up on the stage before anyone could stop him. Two Deliriums were about to step in but the Hooded Figure stopped them. He had to show he wasn't frightened in front of this vast adulating crowd. The Figure still had his arms raised and the cloak had slipped back to reveal the same pentagram mark, in exactly the same spot. Ben pointed to it and then held up his own arm. This confused most people, who couldn't see, but those at the front started to whisper and point, and word soon got back to the rest.

"Show them who you are," said Ben quietly.

The Mathematician tried to stop him, but the Hooded Figure waved him away and pulled down his hood to reveal the face of – Ben Hartley. People gasped. Ben looked at himself. He understood now why he was chosen. It was his dream self that had caused all the trouble and risen to dizzying heights of power in DreamTown, so it was him who had to come and try to stop the terrible Takeover that was still happening.

DreamTown Ben smiled.

"Once you are sacrificed there will only be me, the DreamTown Ben Hartley, and I'll be more powerful. The Harrowing will be secure. Think what an honour it is for you. We thank you."

"But hunting and killing all those people and turning 'em into zombies. It's horrible," said Ben.

His hand touched something in his pocket. He took it out. It was the notebook he'd found in Richmond Park. *Language is a weapon too.*

"Look. This was someone you hunted down like they was just rubbish. Some bloke called James Madison. Just a bloke, but you …"

Someone pushed forward in the crowd. A woman with a sad face.

"James Madison was my husband's name. That's his little notebook. How did you get it? He died in his sleep. Peacefully."

"No. He didn't. Listen," said Ben, "*If anyone finds this, please tell my wife what I should have told her: that I love her more than life itself. What they are doing here in DreamTown is terrible – killing and hunting people.* James Madison, 124 Coleville Terrace, Bradford."

The woman looked accusingly at DreamTown Ben. A small ripple of dissent started. DreamTown Ben raised his hand and the noise stopped.

"Anyway, if you kill me, you'll die yourself," said Ben.

"What are you talking about?" asked DreamTown Ben.

"Everything needs a reflection, a shadow. It's some scientific thing about matter and anti-matter. If they come together they just explode. Once Waketime becomes just a part of DreamTown it'll all go up like the biggest bomb in the universe. Ask them!"

He pointed at Oswald and the Mathematician, who looked distinctly uncomfortable. DreamTown Ben looked at them.

"What is he talking about?"

"Nothing," said Oswald. "He's not a scientist. He's an imbecile. He doesn't know what he's saying."

"It's just a possibility," said the Mathematician. "A remote theoretical possibility."

DreamTown Ben's eyes darkened to thunder. The crowd was starting to turn as unease snaked though it. He'd come too far to back off. There was nowhere to back off to. He nodded at two Deliriums, who grabbed the hapless Oswald and the Mathematician, and dragged them away. DreamTown Ben smiled at the crowd.

"Scientists. Scaremongers. Who needs them? Not us. We know that DreamTown will last for a billion years. We'll live forever. We can be safe forever."

"No you can't," said Ben. "No one's safe forever. Everything changes, and gets scary. This world's called DreamTown. What happens to dreams? They stop when you wake up. And ... *what is it? What is it?* ... Yeh, we're such stuff as dreams are made of. If we're made of dreams and they're made of us, they have to change, and us with it. Nothing stays the same."

Ben was starting to get through to some people. He could feel it.

"That's because you aren't one of the Chosen. We are," said DreamTown Ben.

He beckoned and a Delirium came forward with a large, shining sword. Two Nomads grabbed Ben and held him up. DreamTown Ben nodded and the Delirium lifted the sword. Ben saw that he meant to cleave him in two, straight down the middle. He hoped it would be quick.

Chapter Thirty Two

The Delirium smiled as he held the sword aloft, then the smile turned to surprise as a crack was heard, and a small red hole appeared in his forehead. He stayed perfectly still for a moment, then fell backwards stone dead. From the crowd a raggedy, rope haired figure emerged, holding an old flintlock pistol. The Hermit. He got on the stage and faced the DreamTown Ben.

"I'll be your sacrifice," he said. "Let the boy go."

DreamTown Ben looked baffled.

"No. Dad. Don't do it," said Ben.

DreamTown Ben smiled.

"Ah. I see," he said. "Father and son. Touching."

"Your father too," said Ben.

DreamTown Ben's eyes faltered, but then he gestured to another Delirium, who picked up the sword and raised it. Ben's Dad smiled and took another pistol from his pocket. He aimed it at the Delirium, then suddenly turned and fired at DreamTown Ben, who fell back under the impact, and sat on the floor looking down in astonishment as a red stain spread across his chest. He now looked like a scared little boy instead of a genocidal tyrant. Ben felt a searing pain in his own chest too, but strangely, it felt like something being released. As the stain spread and DreamTown Ben's eyes flickered towards being closed forever something strange was happening outside. The Great hall became lighter as the sun rose. The sun never shone in DreamTown, but here it was. It terrified everyone. The Deliriums hunched against the walls in terror. Only the Nomads, too thick to realise the enormity of what was happening, were unaffected.

On the big screen above the stage everyone saw what was happening. The great exodus to DreamTown had stopped and there was a turning back. It was confused, and a lot of living things didn't know which way to go, but the tide was turning.

Ben's dad turned around. His eyes looked strong and clear and full of love.

"Son. Get out. Live. Please. For me. For your Mum."

Ben jumped off the stage as the sword came down swiftly on his Dad. A great cry went up and some people ran to get on the stage, others ran to escape from the Great hall. All was noise and confusion. The sun continued to rise and send bold lights flashing through the hall. Ben looked on the stage and saw his Dad on the floor, a terrible gash across his throat, another across his chest, but beneath the wrinkles and dirt and whiskers he looked like someone Ben vaguely remembered and loved from when he was little. Two Nomads were pushing through the crowd towards Ben, both holding hatchets. Ben crouched in the crowd and started to move away, then he saw spots of blood leading beneath the stage. He followed them, around the side, pulled a loose plank of wood away where the blood spots stopped, and crept through into the dust and dirt, hearing the thunder of feet on the stage above.

A meaty smell. Damp fur. Blood. He came upon Wolf lying on his side, breathing heavily, tongue lolling bloodily from the side of his mouth. One ear completely torn off, one eye a bloody mess, one front leg mangled and broken, a rib sticking out horribly through his chest.

Ben stroked his head, his muzzle. The first time he had ever done this. His Dad was gone, and now Wolf … he couldn't bear it.

"You can't … *don't say die* … stay in this scabby old hole. You're a hero," he whispered.

Wolf slid his one good eye across Ben, chuckled, and spat in the dust.

"Ain't no heroes, chickadee. We's all just lifestuff breezing downriver to the Reaper," here coughing a little blood.

"I want to go with you," said Ben.

"Not your time yet. Now this DreamTown put right I be skuz-guggling them wild hunts all through the stars. The big eternal. See me sky chasing. Time for a smoke."

He flipped a cheroot in his mouth with his one good paw, then flinted a spark from his claw, but his leg suddenly went into spasm, then became still. The spark landed in the dust, glowed, and died.

Ben buried his face in the warm, smelly fur of Wolf's neck and sobbed until he was empty. Then he fell into the deepest sleep he'd ever known.

Chapter Thirty Three

A blade of sunlight lay golden from the chink in the curtains across the faded carpet and pointed at Ben's neck. It crept further onto his cheek and he awoke with a start. He reached automatically for his inhaler, but his chest was quiet, his breathing slow. Although he didn't know it, he would never suffer another asthma attack. Looking around, everything was the same, everything was changed. He looked at his arm. The pentagram mark was gone. How could that be? *Was this yet another dream*, he wondered. As if to confirm it wasn't the door opened and his Mum came in with a cup of milk and a biscuit. She smiled. There didn't seem much point in saying anything to her about last night. Not yet anyway.

"He's in the garden," she said.

Ben looked at her. Who was in the garden? Then, with a yelp and a hi-de-hoop jump on the bed Scrap was suddenly there, wet and warm and licking Ben's face with mad love. Ben held the little dog tight and felt the night in his head receding. He was here. With his Mum. With Scrap. This was real.

The next night he didn't sleep at all. He got up and looked out at the stars, wondering if anything was real. *We are such stuff* ... The clear night sky. There, far away but close enough to touch, was a slinky, sinewy, figure, like a comet, chasing the stars and whatever else there was to hunt into eternity. Ben fancied he could even see and smell the cheroot. "But," he said aloud, "I wish you was here with me."

A week later Ben walked along the river path with Scrap. It had been an odd week, remarkable because it was normal. Ben hadn't dreamt once. Perhaps now his dream self was dead he couldn't dream. He'd decided not to tell his Mum about his

Dad. What would be the point? There were some things you just had to keep to yourself, or let go. He was so lost in thought he didn't see the figure on the bench, exactly where Jack used to sit to catch his breath.

"Dad," he whispered.

This couldn't be.

His Dad smiled. He still looked a mess, raggedy hair and beard, torn t-shirt, a fresh scar on his throat. Anyone would have taken him for a tramp. Ben sat down heavily, tears welling. His Dad put a scrawny comforting arm around him. As if answering Ben's unasked question, he said: "I don't know how I got here, Ben. I just woke up on the bench, and I knew you'd be along some time."

Ben looked at him.

"Will you stay?"

His Dad looked at the river, at Scrap sniffing some interesting nettles that another dog had recently visited.

"I wish I could say yes. I really do. I'd like to ... just be here. For you. See your Mum and apologise. But I don't think I can. I'll be taken back, next time I sleep, and this time it'll be for good. I just wanted to see you one more time. Wishing is a kind of power, I suppose. So I got this ... visit."

They held each other. Ben leaned into him and closed his eyes. It was all too much. But it was something. It meant something. He opened his eyes and started to ask one of a thousand questions, but he was alone. His Dad was gone. In the Tunnel. Back to DreamTown. Gone. Ben wanted to cry for a week, but Scrap was yapping and raring to go. Ben trudged after him, his mind so full he didn't see them until he almost bumped into them.

Blocking the path a few metres ahead, in the shadows of a bridge, was an older boy, with a bull mastiff. The boy had a shaved head, tattoos on his bare arms. *He's a Nomad – No, that's over.* Normally Ben would have turned around and avoided any potential trouble, but he kept walking. It wasn't that he had suddenly become brave, but that he had become fed up to the gills with being frightened. *Swallow your scared.* And he had just seen his Dad. The bull mastiff growled. Scrap would be hiding in the bushes behind him somewhere, tail between his legs. But suddenly here was little Scrap bounding in front of Ben and squaring up to the larger dog, showing his teeth and snarling meanly. The mastiff growled again, but looked uncertainly at his master. The older boy nodded and the two of them stood aside for Ben and Scrap. Once past them Scrap looked up at Ben and his eyes slid like red gold and Ben felt sure he could smell rotten meat, cheroots and something he'd rather not think about. Then Scrap was gone, chasing up the path towards some new, impossibly exciting escapade.

The End

In an hilarious riot of a tale that echoes an imploding real world, author Steve Attridge introduces scary security guards Baz and Dave; sex-mad failed poet Damion Dimmuck; Dr Duff with his paranoid terror of sick people; Mercedes Blonk, seducer of young men and radical theorist; and psychopathic dwarf, General Spinelli, a bloodstained South American dictator who enrols (at a price) to read (but misunderstand) classic literature.

Unlikely champions of human values are a befuddled academic whose only friends are literary characters, a weedy fantasist student addicted to list-making, and his secret love, the Rubenesque, silent and unsmiling girl with poetry in her soul and a huge cache of illicit chocolate bars under her bed.

At stake are all future generations in the western world ... will they be educated or programmed?

paperback ISBN:978-1-906609-28-3
ebook ISBNs:978-1-906609-29-0

Brotherly Love
by Peter Tomlinson

'Brotherly Love' is the mighty flagship of the renowned Mercy Fleet, financed by one of the richest men on earth to bring emergency relief and medical aid to crippled countries ravaged by poverty, drought, famine and disease ... at least that's what the world believes.

But love and mercy are far from the true mission of the 'Brotherly Love' and its angelic armada. And aged multi-billionaire Vival – internationally praised for his philanthropy – is anything but a selfless humanitarian.

Nearing retirement, Ralph Collingwood has his quiet life in a peaceful English village torn apart when he's ordered by British intelligence bosses on a last desperate international assignment ... to risk his life in a bid to expose what the cargo of the 'Brotherly Love' really is ... misery, torture and death ... and the Mercy Fleet's sinister mission ... to rip the civilised world asunder.

Tomlinson's race-paced thriller spans the wild seas and desolate peaks of the world and of the human spirit as actual brotherly love strives to expose Vival and his Mercy Fleet's sinister plans for the horrendous evil they are.

EPUB: 978-1-927086-18-6
MOBI: 978-1-927086-19-3
PDF: 978-1-927086-20-9

Black Cow
by Magdalena Ball

Freya and James Archer live the high life in a luxury home in Sydney's poshest suburb, with money, matching Jags, two beautiful teenage kids ... and they couldn't be more despondent.

James wakes weeping each morning, dreading the pressures of a long and grueling work day ahead, and Freya is struggling with her foundering real estate career.

Global recession is biting in Australia, and the Archers are afraid.

In a desperate bid for happiness and security they shed the fragile trappings of success and cruise over into the slow lane to take an unmapped turn-off on a country road and live off the land in a remote old farmhouse on the peaceful southern island of Tasmania.

But is this an end to their old misery or the beginning of an even greater one?

The rich poetic and literary quality of Ball's second novel delves into the lives of very real characters as they dig deeply into both the earth and into themselves to discover where their heartaches are really buried.

Fast-paced, gorgeously-written and stunningly perceptive, Black Cow is not only a great read; it is a timely and important one. Joan Schweighardt. Gudrun's Tapestry and other novels

A novel of our time. We follow the characters through all the compromises, adjustments and hard choices that must be made in hopes of a life of wholeness and integrity. This is a life affirming story. Judy Johnson. The Secret Fate of Mary Watson

A masterpiece. Ball's seamless exploration of the faulty human-condition and the urgent notion that money means success is brilliantly interwoven with the gentle quietness of unconditional love, invoking the realization that life is precious, and small enough to cradle in the palm of a baby's hand. Jessica Bell. String Bridge and Twisted Velvet Chains.

paperback ISBN: 978-1-927086-46-9
ebook ISBNs: EPUB : 978-1-927086-47-6
                MOBI: 978-1-927086-48-3
                PDF: 978-1-927086-49-0